DO NOT REMOVE
CARDS FROM POCKET

THE FALCON'S WING

 *A Richard Jackson Book*

THE FALCON'S WING

Dawna Lisa Buchanan

ORCHARD BOOKS • NEW YORK

"The Child on the Shore" from *Hard Words and Other Poems* by
Ursula K. Le Guin, copyright © 1981 by Ursula K. Le Guin,
is reprinted on page ix by permission of HarperCollins
Publishers.

Orchard Books
387 Park Avenue South, New York, NY 10016

Manufactured in the United States of America
Book design by Mina Greenstein
The text of this book is set in 12 pt. Fournier.
10 9 8 7 6 5 4 3 2 1

Library of Congress Cataloging-in-Publication Data
Buchanan, Dawna Lisa.
The falcon's wing / by Dawna Lisa Buchanan.
p.   cm. "A Richard Jackson book."
Summary: After her mother's death, twelve-year-old Bryn
tries to make a new life when her taciturn father moves them
to a rural community in Canada to live with her elderly aunt
and her cousin Winnie, a loving girl with Down's syndrome.
ISBN 0-531-05986-3.   ISBN 0-531-08586-4 (lib. bdg.)
[1. Down's syndrome—Fiction.   2. Mentally
handicapped—Fiction.   3. Family life—Fiction.
4. Farm life—Fiction.   5. Canada—Fiction.]   I. Title.
PZ7.B8766Fal   1992   [Fic]—dc20   91-22545

To Frances and Bill and Frances
for life and love.

Thank you.

THE CHILD ON THE SHORE

Wind, wind, give me back my feather
Sea, sea, give me back my ring
Death, death, give me back my mother
   So that she can hear me sing.

Song, song, go and tell my daughter
Tell her that I wear the ring
Say I fly upon the feather
   Fallen from the falcon's wing.

Ursula K. Le Guin
Hard Words and Other Poems

1

I T was late afternoon when we pulled into the village of Kenmore, Ontario. We'd been driving for two days and had to spend twenty minutes more cruising up and down the main street, looking for Pearl's house. Since I'd never met her, I didn't know what to expect, but already things weren't looking good.

If you've ever been to Kenmore, you'll know you can drive through it several times in twenty minutes. It has one real street dividing a clump of old houses that begin very suddenly and peter out at the bridge over the Castor River. A low rise sits past the bridge, with a tiny schoolhouse perched on the right, and that's it—the end of Kenmore.

My father stopped the truck near a general store.

"Go and ask where she lives," he said, nodding toward it. He climbed out of the truck and started to roll a cigarette.

"Oh." He smiled quickly, then handed me a dollar. "Get a pop, too."

It felt strange to be standing in a street so faraway

from Circleville, Ohio. My legs were still trembling from the hours in the truck, and the cracked pavement of the sidewalk seemed to roll, just a little, under my feet.

I walked toward the store. A boy came slamming out of the door, his arms full of grocery bags. I tried to move past him, but he stepped in front of me, staring.

"Hi," he said.

"Hi."

He looked at my feet, my overalls, my face, but he did not speak again. He was dirty. His face was covered with smudges, and his thick black hair stuck up in spikes. A smear of what looked like tomato sauce ran down the ragged edge of his flannel shirt. His toes were hanging out of one shoe; the other looked like it might burst open at any moment.

A young woman—she looked Indian—came from the store, holding a baby on one hip and a bag of groceries on the other. She was so beautiful I thought of princesses in fairy tales. Her dark eyes turned to me. "Hello," she said, smiling. She had an accent: French, I think. "Cecil, will you help me with this?"

The boy took a few steps away, pulling his own bags closer to his chest.

"I have to deliver these to Mrs. Pisgah. I can't carry any more," he said.

"You could just drop this off on the porch."

"Aw, Leila, I'm working. What more do you want?"

"Cecil!" a shrill voice called.

"Coming, Mrs. Pisgah!" the boy shouted. He jerked

2

his head around at me for one last look, then spun off down the street. I noticed his pants were ripped up the back of one leg so that the cloth flapped as he ran.

The woman sighed.

"I could help, if it's not too far," I offered, taking the bag from her.

"It's just there," the woman said, pointing. There was no jewelry on her slender hand. I suddenly thought of the flash of rings and bracelets my mother always wore. The memory was vivid for a moment, then faded. I looked back at my dad. He was still watching the sky and smoking. He began blowing smoke rings. The little circles popped out of his mouth and floated toward the sky. Without looking at me, he waved his hand, so I knew it was all right to help the woman. I carried the groceries across the street to a small house.

"That's fine, just on the porch," the woman told me, climbing the steps. The baby peeked at me through a stream of black hair. "Thank you for helping. I'm Leila Barton."

"That boy sure was rude," I said.

"He's my son—that is, my stepson. He didn't mean anything by it." She smiled again.

Before she could ask my name, I said, "See you," and turned back to the store. I got up the steps this time, but the door opened again. I hadn't seen a soul while we were driving up and down the street, so this sudden spurt of traffic was a surprise.

The woman who started past me was wearing blue work overalls. Her hair was cut like a man's—short behind her ears and shaved close to her neck around the back—and sprinkled with streaks of gray. She had on a pair of black high-top sneakers, the kind boys in Ohio wear to play basketball. I might have thought she was a man, except for the spotless white cotton blouse she wore, soft and embroidered with intricate white threads along the collar and sleeves. Her eyes were large and blue, and they were fixed on mine like the headlights of an oncoming car.

I decided to give up on the store.

"Excuse me...."

"Yes?" She hoisted the large burlap bag she was carrying from one shoulder to the other.

"Do you know where Pearl MacDonald lives?"

"Yes."

There was a moment then when I thought she wasn't going to say anything more.

"Who wants to know?" she asked, staring at me.

"I do," I said. "I mean, my father and me." I looked over at Dad. He was grinding his cigarette out.

"I'm Pearl," she said. "What's your name?"

"Bryn, Bryn Cameron. And David, my father."

"Oh. David," she said sharply, looking his way. "That's David." She just stood there for a minute, watching him, and then she asked me, "Where's your mother?"

Pearl stared at me, and I stared back hard.

"She died," I said.

She grabbed my arm suddenly and marched me over to Dad in quick time.

"David," she shouted, "you didn't tell me you had a daughter."

We followed Pearl in the truck. She wouldn't get in with us but just turned and marched to the very end of a dirt side road. Then she stuck her head in my father's window. Her face was very pale.

"You didn't tell me Julia was dead. You didn't tell me you had a daughter," she said again. Her eyes were cold, and her mouth trembled. She looked too old to be my mother's sister. I didn't want to get out of that truck, but I was so tired I almost fell out when Dad came around to open my door.

He made me wait on the front porch of Pearl's big old farmhouse. They stepped into the kitchen and started whispering. I leaned up against the door, trying to look like I was just relaxing there, but I listened.

"Why didn't you ever write about the girl?"

"Julia did all the letter writing," my dad said softly. "I didn't know she never told you about Bryn, but if she didn't it must have been because of that business between the two of you so long ago. Jul . . . she died this June. I wanted to come and tell you myself."

But when he started telling her, I could hear Pearl's breathing—hard and dry—then crying that had an ugly sound to it. I moved away from the door and sat on the steps to wait. Her weeping made me uncomfortable, scared all over again.

Dad came out in a minute, but he walked right past me and down to the barn. He does most of his talking to horses, singing them nonsense rhymes and murmuring "tickle" words of encouragement into their ears. He'd made his living in Ohio by training horses.

I always went to my mother when I needed to talk. It already seemed like forever since the last time. In another minute Pearl appeared at the door, her face red and wet. She jerked her hands at me to show I was to come in the house. She didn't try to hug me. I was glad.

"I'll get a room ready for you," she said in a strained voice. "Here's Winnie, my daughter."

Well, no one had mentioned Winnie to me. She was the strangest-looking person I'd ever seen, although that's not saying much after that Cecil kid and Pearl.

There was definitely something wrong about Winnie. She was as skinny as Pearl, but she was tall, like my father. Her hair was straw yellow and stringy. She had slanted green eyes, very far apart. They had little tucks of skin folded over them at the inside corners.

Just by looking you could tell she wasn't like most people. I guess I'm not like most people either, but I don't think you can tell by looking.

She was making supper when I came in. She didn't say a word the whole time she was putting dishes and food on the table, but she kept peeking at me, moving her head from side to side as if she could see only half of me at a time. I stood there, exhausted from our trip, and watched her.

Pearl came back into the kitchen and told Winnie to ring the bell. Winnie giggled, ducked out the door, and pulled a rope hanging from the roof. A rich peal of sound rolled down toward the barn, and within moments my father was at the door. We all sat down at the table.

I reached for my fork, but Pearl made her hand into a stop sign.

"Bless us, O Lord, for these thy gifts," she prayed. I looked over at Dad. He didn't bow his head. When she was finished, the meal began.

I couldn't eat much, but I could see that Winnie had a good appetite. I couldn't understand how she could be so thin if she ate that much food all the time. Pearl handed around plates of chicken, potatoes, beans, apple preserves, fresh bread, butter, a milk jug, and cups of hot tea. Winnie served herself a generous amount of everything, cleaned her plate, and began all over again. Sometimes she leaned over the table so far her hair hung into her potatoes. I wanted to stop looking, but she was right across from me. Her green eyes were fixed on mine even as she pushed another piece of bread into her mouth. It wasn't that she did anything really gross, but having someone stare at you and eat with such intensity was like watching someone pat her head and rub her belly at the same time—just strange. I began to feel a little sick. No one spoke.

After the meal, Dad went out to unload the truck, Winnie started to clear the dishes, and Pearl filled a plastic tub with hot water from a kettle sitting on the back of the wood stove. She put the tub in the old enamel sink, then swirled in some soapy bubbles.

"Dish towels are in there," she told me, her eyes riveted on a drawer in the kitchen table. Silently, I dried as she passed the dishes to me. Winnie swept the floor and went out.

"Aunt Pearl?" I tried.

"You just call me Pearl," she said gruffly. "Hand me that pitcher, will you?"

I guess meeting a twelve-year-old girl is a hard way to find out you're an aunt. She didn't seem interested in anything about me or my life, and in fact didn't say another word. It was harder than ever to imagine her being my mother's sister. My mother's face moved as she listened, frowned, smiled, reflected any story I told her before she thought about it out loud. Pearl's face was like stone. When we finished, the kitchen gleamed in the darkening summer evening.

"Winnie will show you where you sleep," she said finally. "I'm sure your father will be in soon."

I looked out the kitchen window. I could just make out the general store at the end of the road. Winnie was coming up the steps onto the porch with a fistful of dandelions. She zipped past me and disappeared down the hall before Pearl turned around from hanging up her dish towel.

In a moment Winnie was back.

"Take Bryn to the spare room," Pearl said. "And don't dawdle in there."

Winnie giggled, a squeaky, irritating sound. I followed her up a narrow flight of stairs into another hall with four doors along one side; she took me to the door at the far end. I turned the knob and walked into a stifling room.

A huge window, close to the floor, filled most of the far wall. I flung it open and, by kneeling on the faded rug, could see a thick fir tree growing at the corner of the house. I could see Pearl and my father standing on a worn footpath curling down to the barn and the river beyond. I turned back to the room, but Winnie was gone. I hoped I wouldn't see her again soon.

Relieved, I fell on the bed. It was covered with a crocheted blanket and, beneath that, a very old patchwork quilt. I smelled lavender in the stiff sheets. There was a bookcase on the far wall. On the bedside table were a goosenecked lamp and a goldfish bowl jammed full of dandelions, the stalks so massed together that bits and ends had folded up flat against the side of the glass. It looked like something a little kid would give her mother.

"Bryn," my dad said, knocking on the door and surprising me. "Here you go." He dropped a pile of clothes on the bed and eased my mother's books to the floor, then sat down beside me and began rolling a cigarette.

"Thanks," I said.

"Pearl's got three horses," he said, "and twelve milk cows. It's a small farm, but a lot of work for an old woman. Enough to keep me busy."

I didn't care about Pearl's old cows or her old horses or her old farm.

Dad licked the thin paper he held in his hand and smoothed it shut in one swift flick of his fingers. He stuck the cigarette in his mouth, but he didn't light it. Instead, he looked out the window.

"Everything's going to be all right," he said, but it sounded like a question.

"Dad?"

"Yes?"

"Dad . . ."

"What is it, Bryn?" He sounded sleepy.

"Are we going to stay here?"

"We might. We'll see how it goes," he said.

I didn't know how to say all I wanted to know.

"Dad, what's wrong with Winnie?" I asked finally.

"She's impaired, or maybe the word is disabled," he said, tapping the cigarette against his knee. "Pearl had her late in life. That's often risky. Something may have gone wrong when she was born, or she might have been like that from the start." He looked at me for a moment, but then his eyes wandered back to the window.

"So . . . you knew about Winnie?" I asked. I wondered why he hadn't told me. He didn't answer me. "Dad . . ."

"Mmhh?"

"What am I going to do here? Pearl is so bossy. I don't know how to act."

"Just be yourself, Bryn," he answered.

"But I've never lived with anyone besides you and . . . and Mom. I feel strange."

"Don't look back, Bryn," was all he said. "We can't

10

change the past." That didn't exactly answer my question.

"But, but what's going to happen?" I felt like crying.

"We're just going to keep on," he said. He gave my hand a squeeze. I felt like he wanted me to stop asking questions, and that scared me because maybe I wouldn't have the courage to ask him again.

"I want . . . I want things to be the way they were before," I said, miserable. Inside me was a baby song: I want my mother, I want my mother.

"Well, that can't be," Dad snapped, and now he looked angry, too, in the dimming light. He fiddled with his cigarette.

"I'm scared."

"Me, too," he said, and that was the end of the talking. I didn't know the rules for talking with him—what was okay and what wasn't. And he didn't give me any hints. I just knew, by his face, that he wasn't going to say anything else.

We sat there a little longer. I heard the stairs creak and the sound of a door closing softly. Dad stood up.

"Good-night, then," he said, as if we'd been talking the whole time. "See you in the morning."

Sighing, I lay down on the floor and looked out the window. Whiffs of manure, hay, and some fragrant flowers came floating up to me. Then the screen door slammed, and I could smell the smoke from my father's cigarette as he started down the footpath. It was August of the longest summer I'd ever known. I had never felt so lonely in my life.

DREAM

      I AM IN A CORNFIELD. My mother is far ahead of me in the same tall row. Her scarlet dress is half-covered with a shawl of sunflower yellow. She is running.

    "Mom! Mom!"

    No sound is coming out of my mouth even though I am shouting. I am running.

    She stops, looks back at me. A moment skips past. Her face is sad. She shakes her head.

    "Mom! Mom!" Can she hear me? I race forward, but she is gone. The corn is too tall. I am lost.

    I wake up, wet with fear. My mouth is dry. I am in Pearl's house, alone in my dark room.

    "Mom," I whisper. I don't think anyone hears me.

2

A FAT field mouse was sitting on my pillow. I've seen plenty of mice, but I wasn't used to waking up with one.

A long white arm snaked around the door, followed by Winnie's curious, flat face. She whistled. The mouse blinked, then scampered over and climbed up one leg of her overalls. It disappeared into the pocket at her waist. Then the two of them were gone in one soft rustle.

When I came down to breakfast, no one was in the kitchen. The room seemed to be waiting. A bowl of blackberries stood on the table beside an old-fashioned flip toaster, a loaf of homemade bread, and a plate of butter. There was a pot of tea in a crocheted cozy next to a cup and saucer Mom would have cherished. I got some milk from the fridge and filled my cup with it and ate to the singing of birds. Still, no one showed up.

I went to the barn to look for Dad. The two main doors were swung wide, but darkness swelled about halfway down. Three bicycles were leaning against the wall.

" 'Morning, Bryn," Dad called. He was hauling two pails of frothy milk into the sunlight. It figured that Pearl wouldn't have a milking machine.

" 'Morning."

I saw a shadow move behind him, take shape, and become Winnie sprinting through the barn. She disappeared into the darkness.

One of the bikes was a beauty. It was old, like everything else I'd seen on the farm, but tall and black with high handlebars and huge wheels. It looked like a circus bike for clowns. I pulled it out.

"I'm going to ride this," I told Dad. He had a bit of straw in his hair and he looked tired. He put the buckets down and stretched, taking deep breaths. I wondered if he'd slept in the barn.

"Dad, do you want to come exploring with me?" I asked, hoping he'd say yes. But he didn't.

"I can't right now, honey," he told me, picking up the pails again. The straw had fallen out of his hair. "I've got work to do here. You enjoy yourself."

"When are we going to look around?" I asked, trying to make my voice light and careless.

"We'll get to it," Dad said, starting toward a shed beside the barn. He already seemed to belong on the farm, just as he belonged to the stables in Ohio. "You're a big girl. You go on."

I squeezed my eyes shut, not wanting him to see me cry. But it didn't matter—he didn't look back.

"See you later." My voice sounded like a shout in my ears. Dad was already gone.

I jumped on the bike and wobbled down the cement

14

ramp from the barn. The bike was stiff under my body, and I had to spread my arms wide to get a solid hold on the handles, but I felt tall and light on that crazy high seat. Pearl was standing on the porch and smiled when she saw me pedal into the yard.

"How does it fit?" she asked.

"Too big. But I love it."

She nodded. "You can ride it whenever you like," she said, "but Bryn . . ."

Winnie came around the corner of the house just then, pushing another of the barn bikes.

"Time to talk about things later, I guess," Pearl said.

Winnie climbed on her bike and rode up beside me, sticking her legs out on either side to stop. I couldn't believe how silly she looked. Winnie was big, and the bike was small, one a seven-year-old might ride. She started a lazy circle around me.

"Where have you been this morning?" Pearl asked her.

"Barn," Winnie said, grinning at her mother.

"I hope you didn't get in David's way," Pearl said sternly.

"Fun." Winnie was still smiling. I felt a pang of jealousy. Winnie had been hanging around with Dad, probably the whole time I was sleeping. She was a stranger, but he'd already spent more time with her here than he had with me. Maybe you have to like barns to get any attention, I thought. Maybe to him Winnie is just another horse! This thought cheered me up a bit.

"It's trained," she said, and stopped circling. She had

15

a peculiar hiss that sounded after all her *s*'s. Like steam escaping a tight place. Her voice didn't seem to fit her body. Nothing about her fit. She talked like a little kid, but she had to be older than me.

"What's trained?"

"The mouse," Winnie said. "Two mice." She smiled again.

I didn't like looking at Winnie. Instead, I looked at Pearl. She was standing very still on the porch.

"I'm going for a ride," I said then, "and I want to go alone." Kenmore was a small place. It wouldn't take me long to check it out.

"Ride, too. I show you around." Winnie started pedaling. Too sweet, too smiling, all trusting, and curious.

"No."

"Yes, yes, Pearl," Winnie whined, contracting her pale brows. She dug her feet abruptly into the ground, unfolded herself from the bike, and tugged at my sleeve.

"Please, ride, too!"

"Leave me alone," I said, pulling away from her.

Winnie threw her bike on the ground and screamed.

"Winnie, that's enough," Pearl warned. She marched down the steps and stood with us. "Pick up your bike and stop that screaming right now, or you will stay home."

What did she mean by that? Who was Pearl to decide if Winnie would come with me or not?

Winnie bent down for her bike instantly. Her face

16

was smooth again, and she smiled at me. I frowned back at her.

"Bryn," said Pearl, "let her ride with you."

Great! A giant baby riding around with me in my new country. "She won't hurt me, will she?" I asked.

"No," Pearl and Winnie said together, as if other kids had asked before me. Pearl's face had a frosty edge to it. She was small, but I knew I didn't want to tangle with her. Especially not on my first day. I pushed the pedal with my foot and took off as fast as I could, careening down the dirt road, back wheel slipping on the stones. I figured I'd lose Winnie in no time, but she stuck right beside me, riding easily on her tiny wheels. She even hummed a little.

I could see that Winnie was going to be a problem. I could also see that she rode a bike a lot better than I did.

3

CECIL was standing in the street, talking fast to two girls with braids in pretty yellow dresses. A bigger girl sat on the bottom step of the general store, bouncing a small ball and catching it with one hand.

"That's her—there she is," Cecil said when I rode up. I looked behind me. Winnie had stopped to the side. He meant me. The others were looking me over. The big girl snickered.

"I see she found the Snake Girl," she said to Cecil. "Lucky her."

I thought about it. Winnie did look like a snake, sort of. And the way she talked could make you think of snakes hissing.

"Pearl said she should come with me," I began.

"Pearl MacDonald?"

"Yes."

"What's your name?"

"Bryn."

"That's a weird name," the big girl said.

"No weirder than his," I answered, nodding at Cecil.

She liked that. "True!" She laughed, standing up. "I'm Rita Pisgah."

She looked like one of those explorers you see on the cover of history books, bigger than any girl I'd seen. Her skin was pale and freckled. Her hair gleamed red in the sun.

"Are you going to be here awhile?" she asked. "We can show you around. This is Rachel, and this is Virginia. Their mum is Dr. Pulumbo. She works a lot."

The girls didn't open their mouths. They continued to stare at me, like two dolls made of china.

"Twins?" I asked.

"No, Rachel's a year older," Rita said, patting the child's head. "Their dad teaches at Carleton University in Ottawa. I'm the family baby-sitter. The nanny."

I wondered what was wrong with Rachel and Virginia. They certainly looked old enough to talk, but Rita seemed to be their voice.

"Do you go to school?" I asked Rachel. She nodded, unsmiling. I realized she wasn't really looking at me after all. She was staring at Winnie. Winnie hung back by the side of the step. She made a slow soft sound like a sad dog.

"Come on!" Rita commanded, pocketing her ball and heading down the street. "Everybody except the Snake Girl."

"But . . ."

"She's a retard."

"But Pearl said—"

"Pearl, shmearl," Rita said grandly. "Pearl won't

know. Just leave her there. The Snake Girl never tells, do you?"

Winnie whimpered.

"You won't tell, will you?" Rita said menacingly, coming back to lean over Winnie.

"Come on!" Cecil said impatiently.

I didn't care what happened to Winnie, but I didn't want Rita or Cecil bossing me around.

"Who put you in charge?" I asked Rita. She looked past the top of my head, then turned around and started walking again.

"You're from the States, then?" Rita called over her shoulder. Virginia and Rachel hung from her hands like two bunches of bananas.

"From Ohio." I looked back at Winnie, who was pushing her bike more and more slowly behind me.

"I could tell you were from the States," Rita went on. "You talk round. It sounds funny. Now, here's where we go fishing." Keeping a grip on Rachel and Virginia, she clambered down the bank beneath the bridge and stepped out onto a large flat stone. I dropped my bike.

"Do you catch any?" I asked, following her.

"Sometimes," Rita said. "You have to use the right bait."

The Castor River didn't look encouraging for fish life. It was muddy and shallow.

"I used to live near a quarry," I said. "It was fed by a stream and filled with very cold, clean water. It was really deep. My . . . I mean . . . I used to swim in there and take a canoe out on it."

20

Winnie appeared at the bridge with her bicycle.

"Go on, Snake Girl. Run home!" Cecil shouted at her.

Winnie backed up some, but she continued to stand there. Her green eyes looked blank.

"Aw, we'll come back another time and fish," Rita said. "I'm not supposed to have these two down here, anyhow. Sometime, when they're with their mum, we'll come and bring food, hang around, and fish a little." She pulled at Rachel and Virginia, leading them up the bank.

"Yeah, but you won't want to bring her," Cecil said, nodding toward Winnie.

I jumped on my bike. I wasn't sure I wanted to go fishing with them. Or riding with Winnie. Or keep living in Canada. I took off, and Winnie followed me silently, up the hill to the school—a small white building with a bell on the roof. It looked like a faded picture postcard.

"I in the little room," Winnie said when I stopped to look.

"The little room?"

"Two rooms. One for little kids, one for big," Winnie explained. If Winnie was in the little room, I'd probably be in the coat closet. She was at least a foot taller than me.

"You like flowers?"

"Sure, I do," I said.

"Flowers in your room."

I remembered the ball of dandelions. "Those are weeds, Winnie."

21

"Pretty," Winnie said confidently.

"How old are you?" I asked.

"Fourteen. I have two mice."

"You already told me that."

Winnie nodded, hugging herself. She tried again. "You like flowers?"

"Yes, thanks, Winnie," I said grudgingly. "Come on. Your mother will be worried about you."

"Your mother?" Winnie asked. I didn't want to talk about my mother, not to Winnie.

"I'm getting tired," I said. "Let's go."

We pedaled slowly back down the hill and turned at the general store. I could see the men haying in Pearl's front field. They were fairly close to the road. Dad was pitching hay, but when he saw me, he waved. I stopped and waved back. Winnie waved, too. He didn't mean that wave for her, but she had that foolish smile on her face again. I watched the haymaking for a moment and then hopped on the bike. Winnie was already in the house by the time I got to the barn.

4

I N Pearl's mind Winnie and I were a
team. Right from the start she put me
to work beside her. We were like an oddly matched
set of workhorses—tall, thin Winnie with her fair hair
and me, short and thin, dark haired and scowling. That
first lunch we had to peel and boil potatoes, snap and
shell peas and boil them, fry pork chops and open a
jar of apple preserves for the homemade bread, brew
an enormous pot of tea and make a pitcher of lemon-
ade. We set the table, putting cups and saucers and
glasses at each place, and then we sliced a pie. I couldn't
believe it when everything was ready and just the four
of us sat down to eat.

"Winnie?" said Pearl.

"Thank you for the birds that sing. Thank you, God,
for everything," she chanted.

Dad and I looked at each other across the table. I
picked up my fork.

"And thank you, Lord, for sending David and Bryn
to us," Pearl added in a strong voice. I put my fork
down.

"Thank you for this beautiful day. Amen." Pearl looked up. "Pass those potatoes to your father," she ordered.

"We don't say prayers before we eat at home," I mentioned.

"Mrs. Pisgah said her Rita met you today," Pearl said. News traveled fast in Kenmore. I guess Pearl wasn't interested in what we did or did not do in Ohio. "What did you do while you were in the village?"

"We met ... I don't know ... some kids at the general store. We went down to the river."

"I don't want you down at the river, Bryn," Pearl said. "It's dangerous. At times it gets high."

"That river?" I snorted. "It's nothing but a skinny old puddle."

"Skinny puddle it may be now, but it gets deep when we have a lot of rain, and in the spring. That river has flooded many times."

"I know how to handle water," I said, looking at Dad. He was busy with the jar of apple preserves. "This river is nothing compared to the Island Road quarry."

"A quarry is a different beast," Pearl observed. "And Winnie knows she's not allowed at the river."

"I can go, can't I, Dad?"

My father looked uncomfortable.

"Pearl may know best about the river," he said. "We don't know our way around yet. Why don't you wait until I can come with you?"

That made me really mad. I might not be the world's

24

best bike rider, but if there is anything I can do well, it's swim. The Castor River held no danger for me. And how long did my father think I should wait until he had time to come with me? I didn't say a word for the rest of the meal.

Pearl and Dad went out to the barn. Winnie and I had to clear up, and it took a long time.

Winnie must have known I was angry. "Bryn?" she asked. She reached for my arm and stroked it gently. I shook her off.

"Bryn?" she tried again. But I was sick of her.

"You leave me alone," I said bitterly.

"I sorry," Winnie said, looking confused. When she went out to the barn, I couldn't help feeling that everyone out there deserved one another—Dad, Pearl, and Winnie. Let them spend the afternoon in a smelly, dark, old barn. I went to my room to read. I read and read those first few days.

Pearl seemed to have something to say on every subject. She didn't like Dad's smoking. For a week or so she just watched hard when he rolled his cigarettes, but finally she blurted, "David, Earl never smoked."

"Oh?"

"It's not good for you," she said.

"I don't smoke much."

"You won't smoke in the barn? Or in the house?"

"No." In Circleville, Dad smoked in the house but not the stables. Mom told me he would never frighten the horses with smoke.

"Well," said Pearl. "Well."

Then she didn't like the way I did chores.

"Wring out that rag," she instructed from the sink after breakfast one day. "That table needs to be scrubbed again."

For several mornings in a row, she sent me back to my room to remake the bed, until at last I figured out what she meant when she asked me to make hospital corners, with the sheets tucked in a certain way. She made me weed in the garden for a little while every evening; I swept the back porch so many times I thought the broom would wear out.

"You're growing," she commented one day when I came down to breakfast in cutoffs and a short T-shirt. "Those things are too small."

"They're supposed to be like this," I said.

Pearl just rolled her eyes.

She was more patient with Winnie, but she never let her off any work. If Winnie forgot something while setting the table, Pearl told her what to do, step by step, as if she were a toddler.

"Take the biggest spoon, Winnie," she'd say. "No, not that one, the biggest one. There. Now, put that spoon in the bowl with the green beans. Are those green beans? No. There, now you have it. All right, bring the glasses to the table. Winnie, have you forgotten Uncle David's place? Will you get me the pot holder? Fine. Ring the bell now, please."

Yet I could tell she loved Winnie. Every morning she'd kiss her cheek, and often she brushed her hair

26

before letting her sit at the table. At lunchtime she'd take her to the sink to see if her face was clean enough where she'd washed, and if it wasn't, she scrubbed it again with a dishcloth. She tugged at Winnie's hems and picked tiny fluffs from her shirts. There was something tense and hawklike in the way Pearl did these things, as if she thought someone might try to steal Winnie away.

I wondered what Pearl thought of me. She seemed to think I could take any criticism or work assignment she wanted to dish out, but she didn't seem to consider me in any personal way. And she never asked questions. I wondered if she was just too old. It was harder than ever to think of her as my mother's sister.

Mom's meals were simple and quick, easily put together so there was time for other things. She had lots of time for reading, walking, swimming, stuff like that. She always wondered what you were thinking about or how you felt about something or what you wanted to do next. Pearl never asked any of those things. Neither did she hug or kiss or touch me. Not that I wanted that. If she thought of me at all, it seemed to be in terms of what job I should do next.

Pearl, in one day, could accomplish more than I planned for my whole childhood—maybe even my whole life. She always had breakfast on the table in the morning and was last to bed at night after hours of quilting or needlework. In the fields or the barn she flung bales of hay with noisy grunts. She smacked the rumps of cows and pushed them with both hands to

27

get them out of her way, groaning with effort and heaving her entire tiny body along after them. But she left the milking to Dad.

Winnie liked to put her face against the velvet flanks of the cows when she watched him. She hummed tunelessly to them, stroking their wet, pink noses. But she was afraid of the horses.

If Dad gave us some carrots to feed them, she dropped hers on the ground the minute the horse shoved its nose at her hand.

"Bryn! Bryn do it," she'd cry. She watched me carefully as I fed the carrots to Ginger, Snap, and Bauble, but she wouldn't come near. "Big teeth," she said.

Dad laughed watching her, and Winnie ducked her head, her face bright red.

Soon, Winnie was following me everywhere. The closer she stuck, the farther my father seemed to be. I couldn't be alone with him. Since that first day, if I went to the barn to watch him milking or brushing the horses, Winnie would be right behind me. It was like having a shadow bigger than me, a shadow with blonde hair.

Whenever I could get by myself, I kept reading. I had finished with Mom's fairy tale collections and was beginning on her poetry books. There were lots of pieces I didn't understand, but others were exciting or funny. I like the way poetry gives you time to think about what you've just read. They're a lot shorter than stories, so you can read them over again right away. I was outside reading when Pearl tromped onto the porch one afternoon.

"Bryn, help me haul those washtubs up here." She pointed.

"I'm busy," I said.

"You're not as busy as you're going to be if you don't get off your behind and help me," Pearl replied. "Right now."

"Gee, Pearl," I complained, putting my book down. "You're a regular slave driver." I helped her move one sloshing tub, then another. "What are you doing?"

"Dyeing some curtains for your father's room," she answered, swirling in scarlet color with a wooden stick. She had given him the room next to mine.

Pearl hoisted the pale curtains into the water and stirred and stirred. She looked like a tiny witch at a caldron.

"Pearl?"

"What is it, Bryn?"

"Why don't you talk to me? I mean, you talk to me, but it's always about some chore for me to do."

"What should I talk about?"

"I don't know. Stuff. Things about people, or things that happened."

I probably shouldn't have mentioned it. Her face turned stony. "I don't know. I'm not used to that kind of talking, I guess," she said, and she looked surprised. "It's cost me, not being good at talking."

"What do you mean?"

"It cost me your mother's friendship, for one thing,"

she said sadly. "In a way, it cost me her life. I never knew anything more about her after she left here."

Mom had chosen not to tell me about Pearl or Winnie either. Maybe Pearl already knew that. She didn't go on, so I said, "Maybe you could tell me about that time." I picked up another stick and started punching at the heavy curtains.

"Julia married your father when they met in Toronto. Your mother was going to school there," Pearl said. "Your father was visiting friends. She brought him home to Earl and me just after Winnie was born. We had a terrible fight. She wanted me to put Winnie in an institution, said I was too old, that I had a life of my own and that the baby was 'damaged' and were we out of our minds? It hurt me, Bryn. When she left, I was glad. I said I never wanted to see her again."

I looked down at the tub. Pearl was whipping those curtains around like a one-woman typhoon.

"I didn't mean it," she went on. "We began to send Christmas cards and small notes back and forth, but we both were stubborn and we both held a grudge. She never shared important news." She glanced at me. "And I never knew she was sick. All those years wasted. Her fault, and my fault, too. Maybe you can help me," she finished gruffly.

"With what?"

"With talking the way you want to talk," she said. "Your mother was the talker. You must have learned something from her. God knows it wasn't how to keep house. She never cared for that."

30

Pearl groaned as she flopped the heavy mess into the second tub. Red stain began to spread slowly through the clear water. The curtains were bleeding.

"Anything else?" she asked.

"Not just now," I said.

"Hum. Maybe you're not so much of a talker your-self," Pearl said, shooting me a shrewd smile. "No mind. We'll find something to do with each other." She slapped me lightly on the back. "You can get back to your book now, if you like," she said. "Thank you."

I picked up my book and went inside. The house was dark after the bright sun on the porch. As I flopped into a chair, I saw Pearl flinging the curtains over the clothesline. They billowed in the breeze and fluttered like flags with clothespins marching across the tops. Good thing we didn't have a bull on this farm, I thought.

When Pearl called, Winnie came from the barn, eyes squinting. I could tell she had a mouse—maybe two—in her pocket.

"Time to start lunch, Winnie," Pearl said. "We'll do it ourselves today. Just the two of us."

5

WINNIE called her mice Mick and Mike. If Pearl had known they were often in the house—in the kitchen—tucked inside Winnie's overalls, she probably would have died. I didn't think she knew about the mice at all, but one terrible day near the end of August I found out that she did.

After the usual huge noon meal of meat, potatoes, vegetables, dessert—the works—I saw Winnie sweep the bread crumbs off the table and into her other hand. She threw some outside on the grass around the house for the birds, but I knew Mick and Mike were going to get most of those crumbs. Pearl's hay was in, and Dad had gone to help on another farm. Pearl left the kitchen chores to me, but when I'd finished I felt bored and cranky. I was tired of reading, and it was a beautiful warm day. I wandered out to the barn.

Winnie was sprawled on the cement inside the big wooden doors with Mick and Mike scrambling through her fingers. She was clucking and singing to them as if they were dolls.

"Bryn," she sang, her face lighting up when she saw me.

"Can I hold one of them?" I asked. Her face clouded a little. "Come on, Winnie. Just let me hold one, okay?"

Winnie, usually so willing, looked unhappy.

"No," she said slowly. "Mine."

She got up, and the mice chased each other up her leg and into her pocket. Their heads popped out again almost immediately. If I hadn't been feeling mean, I might have laughed.

"Winnie MacDonald, you really are a snake," I hissed at her. "Why won't you let me hold one? I'll be careful."

But she looked doubtful, and meanness burst inside me, turning into something worse. I pushed her, grabbing at her pocket. Winnie pulled away. I felt one of the little creatures slip into my palm for an instant, but it kept on slipping and fell to the cement. For a moment there was pure silence, and then the tiny animal began to scream. I didn't know mice could make such a sound.

"Mick," Winnie wailed. The mouse was bent in a wrong-way curve, a gray smudge at our feet. The sight of it made me frantic.

"Look what you did!" I shouted at her. But it was my fault, and I knew it.

Winnie was crying now, big noisy sobs. "No, Bryn," she said—and fled.

And just as suddenly Pearl was standing there, her hair standing out around her tiny face. She looked down at the mouse. I held my breath.

"Its neck is broken," she said at last. "I'll have to kill it." She picked the mouse up with a shoveling motion of her hand and walked quickly down the length of the barn, fading into the shadows like a queen in overalls. I couldn't hear its screams anymore. Tears scratched at my eyes.

But here was Pearl again, offering me a dead mouse in one of her wrinkled hands. Mick was now a still, disordered weight with fading gray eyes and a frozen, plaintive mouth.

"Bryn," said Pearl. "You have a mouse to bury. And when you're done, you better get started on the laundry."

In a way it was a relief to have work to do then. I didn't want to think. I washed all the sheets, towels, and clothing and hung them on the line to dry. Then I made supper from the noon meal leftovers, set the table, and cleaned out the pantry. The afternoon faded into dusk. I didn't see Pearl or Winnie, and when my father came in to wash he asked me where they were.

I shrugged. "Not sure," I said, turning away from him. I was ashamed and frightened. I didn't know how to tell him what had happened. I dreaded seeing Winnie, but I could hardly stand to be alone with myself. Dad left to look for them. I could hear the clock ticking on the top of the fridge. The potatoes simmered on the back of the stove, and I added more water from the kettle. I saw they were already overcooked. I checked the ham, covered the pan, and pushed it back into the

34

oven. When Dad came in, my heart started to pound and I felt dizzy.

"Bryn," he said softly. "Why did you do that?"

"I don't know," I said, struggling to keep from bursting into tears. He was standing all the way across the room.

"It's not like you to be hurtful," he said. "I didn't think I'd ever have to tell you . . ." His voice petered out.

"Tell me what?" I tried to sound calm. What I had done seemed terrible to me, too. I didn't know what to do to make things better. Maybe Dad could tell me.

"I didn't think I'd have to say that life is about caring for things, not destroying them," he said heavily.

"Like the way you cared for Mom?" I said. I didn't mean to say it; I'm not even sure where the words came from, but like poison on an arrow I saw them stab my father and settle deep inside him.

No one will ever love me now, I thought in despair. I had a sudden picture of myself, dangerous and cold, and I wondered what had happened to me. Dad's face was still, still, but he cleared his throat and walked toward me. I was surprised when he folded me into his arms and hugged me. He stroked the top of my head.

"Try, Bryn," he said. "Please try." I nodded. Pearl and Winnie came in, both looking exhausted.

"Supper's ready," I said timidly. The two of them went to the sink and washed. Pearl asked Dad about the work on the Smiths' farm, and he told her. Winnie sat with her head down at the table. She didn't eat very much, and neither did I. I kept looking at her, hoping she would look back, but she didn't.

"Your turn for dishes, Winnie," Pearl said gently when the meal was finally over. Obediently, Winnie got up to clear the plates. Dad and Pearl went outside. I sat there, fiddling with my fork, staring at an untouched piece of apple pie. Winnie took all the dishes from the table except mine. Then she began the washing up.

"Winnie," I said. "Winnie."

She turned around, still looking somewhere behind me, not at me.

"Winnie, I'm sorry," I said.

She looked at me. Nodded. Turned around again.

"Winnie," I tried again, pushing away from the table and going to the sink. "I really am sorry. I didn't mean to hurt Mick. I wish I could start today all over again."

"Me, too," Winnie said miserably. Tears began to collect in the little pockets at the corner of her eyes. She looked so sad, I couldn't stand it.

My voice was impatient—I knew it. "What can I do to make it better?"

"Pearl said just mouse. Mick just mouse."

"I know," I said. "But you liked him."

"Loved him," Winnie corrected me.

"Yeah."

"Oh, well," Winnie said, sounding just like Pearl. She turned around. She reached into her pocket with damp hands and lifted Mike out.

"Careful," she instructed, pressing the trembling creature into my hand.

36

Mike didn't try to run away, but I folded my other hand over his back just to be sure. He flattened himself out on my palm. I admired him for a moment, feeling the tiny heart racing against my skin. Then I carefully put him back into Winnie's water-reddened hands.

"Thanks," I said, feeling shy.

"We share," Winnie said. She still didn't look happy, but she didn't look quite as tragic as before, either. She plunked him into her pocket again, sweeping some pie crumbs from Dad's plate right in after him.

"Should I help you with the dishes?" I asked, not knowing what else to say.

"Yes," Winnie said.

"I think I'll just eat my pie first," I said, and I went to the table. Every bite of that pie was delicious.

6

"DAVID, Bryn needs clothes for school," Pearl announced. We were eating lunch. "School starts next week."

"We don't have money," my father replied, glancing at me.

"The milk check came today in the mail."

"That's not ours."

"David, you've taken on a lot of the work around here. It's worth more than room and board to me. I want you to have money."

"No." My father's chin was sticking out, and he shut his mouth into a firm little line.

"I won't hear no," Pearl said sharply. "You can't send the girl to school in clothes that climb up her neck. I will sew for her when I get the time, just as I do for Winnie, but there are some things a young lady needs that I can't make for her, like shoes and underwear, and she's going to have them if I have to choke you with the money." She glared at my father. Even though they aren't related by blood, they looked like twins at that moment.

"We aren't taking your money," my father said.

"Just what do you think you are going to do?" Pearl patted the table with the flats of her hands. "Life requires some cash, even if it's not much. Do you think I plan to make a fortune off the sweat from your back?"

"Aren't you exaggerating a little?" asked my father, but he looked more relaxed.

"David, we're going to have to come to some arrangement," Pearl went on more quietly. "You can take a salary or a percentage of our milk and hay money. That way you can be in charge of your own finances without having to come to me, and I'll feel more comfortable."

"Okay," said my father. I was surprised it was settled so quickly.

Winnie and I had left our dishes in the sink and were almost at the kitchen door.

"Stop right there," Pearl ordered. "You and Winnie need to clean up. I mean dresses. And I mean now!"

"But Pearl—"

"No buts. Get up those stairs and wash."

Winnie beat me to the bathroom, but she left the door open, so I went in and scrubbed my face and hands beside her. We both looked up at the wavy mirror over the sink. Our cheeks were bright red, and our hair, slick with water, stuck up around our faces, making us look like pixie children. Winnie began to laugh—a real laugh, a rich, belly-born chuckle that rolled up out of her mouth in waves. Just watching her laugh made me smile. She laughed harder, and then I started laughing, too.

"We look frightened," I snorted between rolls of chuckles. That sent us off again.

"Girls!"

For one frozen moment our faces were frightened, reflected back in the mirror with open mouths, wide eyes, and shocked, electric hair. Then we started laughing again but scooted down the hall to our bedrooms.

"Like lions," Winnie gasped as she shut her door.

Inside my room I stopped laughing right away. I didn't have a dress to wear. I stripped out of my pants and T-shirt and sat, in underpants and socks, on my bed. I looked at my closet. A skirt and blouse hung inside, both too small. There were lots of pants and shirts and my ugly brown loafers. They still fit me, but I hated those shoes.

Pearl glided in onto the bed like a bird making a silent landing. "Not ready yet?" she asked quietly. I stared at her. She had on a peach, silky dress with a belt. She wore stockings and white shoes with low heels. She even had big clip-on earrings with lots of white stones clumped together in a circle. And bright red lipstick.

"I . . . I . . ."

"Haven't got a dress," Pearl finished wisely. She was wearing perfume, too, and the smell of roses filled my room, making it seem hotter than it already was. She didn't say anything about my underwear. "I thought that might be the case. There's an old dress of

40

Winnie's hanging up in the bathroom that will do for now. Come down when you have it on."

I blinked, and Pearl was gone, but her perfume hung in my room like a mist. I sprinted back down the hall and peeked behind the bathroom door. I saw a perfectly respectable white cotton dress, plain but pretty, with a gathered skirt and short sleeves. I put it on. I felt good in that dress. I washed my feet and legs and pulled my loafers onto my bare feet.

Pearl examined me. She said only, "That looks good on you. It's too small for Winnie now."

Winnie turned up in a jumper with a plain white T-shirt underneath. She looked older without her usual overalls. Pearl put Winnie's lank hair up in a ponytail.

We climbed into Pearl's truck, a black, wide-faced thing with a plywood cover over the bed in the back. We drove along Highway 31 for a long time.

When we lived in Ohio, my parents took me up to Columbus about three times a year. We went once to do Christmas shopping, once during the summer for the Ohio State Fair when my father was taking care of Mr. Trenton's show horses, and again to do shopping for my school clothes. Dad didn't like the city, but my mother did. We went only when she was feeling well. She always took me out to lunch, and sometimes to a movie at one of the big cinemas.

"Here we are—Billings Bridge," Pearl said, breaking into my thoughts and turning left from Bank Street into a shopping center. We went into store after store until I found myself, tired and loaded down with boxes and bags, dragging my feet back out to the truck. I thought, Only Pearl could make shopping seem like hard work.

Winnie poked me. "Like stuff?"

I nodded. It was nice to have several outfits to wear, and all of them the right size. Pearl insisted on the kinds of things I had to have—underwear, socks, shoes, and the like, but she let me choose the styles.

"That's enough for one day," she said. "We'll have Leila help sew up a few new skirts."

"Why would she do that for me?" I asked.

"It means a little extra money for her," Pearl said. "Besides, she's the best seamstress in town." My stomach rumbled. We piled into the truck and drove up Bank Street. Streetlights were beginning to flick on, and the traffic had thinned. Pearl drove, and Winnie hummed flatly. I stared out the window, trying to see, but it was getting dark.

We stopped to eat hamburgers, french fries, and milkshakes just outside the city. The waiter plopped a bottle of white vinegar on the table. Pearl and Winnie shook drops of it all over their fries.

"Want some on your chips?" asked Pearl, pushing the bottle over to me.

"No," I said, but I watched as they gobbled theirs down. I just dumped ketchup on mine. I could see the waiter staring at Winnie. I stuck my tongue out at him.

Two days after the big shop, Pearl took us to Winchester, the town where Dr. Pulumbo had her office. This was how I met Rachel and Virginia's mother.

42

She had short, stiff black hair that smelled of hair spray and wore cat-eye glasses. Beneath the frames, if you looked closely, you could see a pair of warm brown eyes, but she was very brisk and didn't waste a minute.

"When you've undressed, put this on," she ordered as soon as Pearl made the introductions. She handed me a cotton sheet with arms and ties. She weighed and measured me, peered into my eyes, ears, and nose, pressed my abdomen, and hammered my knees. She kept making notes on a chart.

"You may begin your menses, your period, soon," she said crisply, handing me a little pamphlet. "Why don't you read this and then ask Pearl, or me next time you visit, if you have any questions."

I felt like a fool. I guess she thought I didn't know anything.

"Is Rita Pisgah really your nanny?" I asked her.

She looked surprised. "I wouldn't call her a nanny, but she is a very good baby-sitter," Dr. Pulumbo answered.

I remembered, then, about fishing.

Winnie had her turn while I waited in the next room. I read the pamphlet from cover to cover. Growing up, it seemed, was getting more complicated by the minute. I didn't want to ask Pearl about any of this stuff.

Winnie burst out of the examining room. Pearl had gone in with her, and she looked upset.

". . . very common with Down's syndrome," Dr. Pulumbo was saying. She touched Pearl's arm. "It's not a decision you have to make right now," she said,

43

"but Pearl, as your physician, it's my responsibility to keep you informed. You can't live forever."

Pearl nodded, and we left.

"What was that all about?" I asked when we were in the truck.

"Dr. Pulumbo thinks I should consider putting Winnie in a group home."

"What's that?"

Winnie sat very quietly, looking at me sideways.

"It's a home where people who need help with living skills live together. Counselors and other staff work with them," Pearl said uneasily.

"What's it like?" I asked.

Winnie shifted around between us in the front seat of the truck.

"Can we talk about this later?" Pearl snapped. She stopped for honey in Vernon.

I waited in the truck with Winnie. She picked up my hand and began counting the lines on it. "Here the house," she said, stroking my thumb, "and here a barn. Oops! I forgot—swimming pool!" She spit into the palm of my hand.

"Yecch!" I pulled my hand away.

Winnie grabbed it back and pressed it against her cheek. "Not live in group home, Bryn," she said, as though she were very old and wise. "Live with Pearl and David and Bryn."

7

PEARL sent me to the general store to get powder for dusting potato bugs. Rita was sitting on the front steps kicking at some dirt.

"What are you doing?"

"I'm waiting for Cecil to finish working," she said, looking up. Her eyes narrowed against the bright sun. "We're going to fish this afternoon. Want to come? We won't get away much after school starts."

"Sure," I said.

"Bring something to eat," she said, looking at her feet again. "And don't bring the retard."

Cecil was nowhere to be seen inside the store. I got the powder and went back outside. Rita was already gone.

Pearl went right to the garden with a pair of gloves, the powder, and an old sifter. I made a tomato sandwich and ran up to my room. Pearl had inspected often enough to make me put most of my things away, but I still had some stuff crammed under the bed. It's funny she never looked there during our hospital corner sessions. I rifled through the pile until I found my knapsack. I put the sandwich in it and went back downstairs.

"Ride, too?" Winnie asked.

"No, I'm on my own today. See you," I told her. I strode away from the house quickly, not looking back. I didn't want Winnie following me.

When I got down to the flat rock, Rita was already there with Cecil and another boy. They looked like they had been there awhile.

"This here's Ed." Cecil made the introduction. "Ed, this is Bryn. She's from the States."

"From Ohio," I said. Ed had white hair and blue eyes and skin as pale as starlight. He looked like those pictures of Christmas angels you see on the covers of children's books.

"Ohio," said Ed. "Hi."

"Got a rod?" shouted Rita. "Didn't think you would. Here, use this one." She handed me a long, willowy stick with thread tied to it. It had a hook on the end. Rita had a soup can full of worms. She held it out for me to see, then put it down on the rock.

Ed and Cecil had real rods, the kind you buy in a store, with metal hoops for the line to run through and a reel with a windup handle. Ed didn't say another thing to me. He sat down on the rock, punched a worm on his hook, and cast the line into the water. He immediately reeled in a glob of weeds. He cleaned it off and cast again. He leaned back a bit.

Rita was busy wrestling a worm onto her hook. The worm didn't want to go, and Rita's hook kept coming untied from the string she was using for a line.

I had no plan for putting a worm on my hook. I don't know why, but I had never gone fishing before in my life and didn't know what to do now.

Rita looked my way, dropped a worm next to me, and said, "Just spear it." The instant the poor worm began to wriggle I felt sick.

"I caught a big catfish here last week," Cecil said. "Mean old thing tried to pull me into the river." He made sure I was watching as he dipped his hand into the can and took out a fistful of worms. He stuffed them into his pocket and whistled.

"You're such a liar, Cecil Barton," Rita said. She was hunched over her worm and hook, tugging and tying.

"I did, too, catch one. Just because you didn't see it doesn't make me a liar," Cecil said.

"Don't get started with me," Rita said. "Just fish, will you?"

Cecil had a worm on his hook by then, but he stood on the rock with the line in his hand. The rod lay beside his feet. He glared at Rita, then turned to me.

"You've never fished before?"

"No."

"I fish all the time. You'll never learn if you don't get the worm on," he offered.

"I can do it." I had to get his mind and his eyes off my worm. "What do you do at the store, Cecil?"

"I deliver groceries, help them stock shelves, clean up. I like it." He glanced at Rita as if expecting her to slap him, but Rita was looking triumphant, molding worm pulp around her hook. She cast her line into the water and turned her back on us.

"I help older folks get their groceries home and sometimes stay to unpack them. I weed out back of the store. I get paid for it. I make quite a bit of money."

"Liar!" Rita hissed. She didn't turn around.

Cecil's face changed color. "Maybe not a lot of money," he said.

I struck upon a plan for managing my worm. I slid it off the rock with the toe of my sneaker and threw my hook into the water quickly. It sank about two inches from the rock, and I just let it hang there. Ed caught my eye and smiled, but he didn't say anything.

We stood, looking into the water, for a long time. No one was catching fish. The sun was hot, and I began to feel sleepy. It didn't seem worth the trouble to be disobeying Pearl and my father to stand on a warm rock by the side of this lazy river, listening to Cecil talk constantly. He told us all about Rachel and Virginia.

"They take lessons, even in the summer," he reported. "Baton, ballet, piano, tap, and singing. Their house is right next to mine. They don't get to go outside much, unless Rita has them. Dr. Pulumbo invites me in sometimes. They have all kinds of stuff in their house. Piles of paper and bowls of crayons, paints and clay and dolls, of course, being they're girls. They have a trunk full of costumes from their dance recitals. They have puppets and games. I don't see how two kids could have all that stuff." Cecil seemed to run out of steam.

Rita shot a meaningful look at me. "Tell her about your house, Cecil," she said.

"What about it?"

"Cecil lives in an Indian house," Rita said.

"I do not," Cecil said scornfully.

"His daddy was an Indian lover!" chanted Rita.

"Shut up! You shut up!" Cecil's voice had gone soft and low.

"Your real mom is dead and gone, dead and gone," Rita went on. "Your daddy moved in with a dirty Indian, didn't he? That squaw food must have killed him, Cecil, so you better watch out what you eat."

Cecil kicked Rita's can of worms into the water. "There," he said. "Let's see you catch a fish now."

Rita remained calm. "Did you bring any food?" she asked me.

If Rita talked about Cecil's family like that, I knew I could never tell her anything about my mother.

"I have a sandwich." It looked a little soggy, so I handed it to her.

Ed reached behind him and pulled a large bag of potato chips from a paper sack. Cecil looked back into the water.

"Bryn." The thin call rolled down the hill to the rock and pulled all three of our heads toward the bridge. Winnie was standing there.

"I thought I told you to leave her," Rita said impatiently.

"I did leave her. Let her come down," I said, feeling uneasy.

"Aw, Bryn, no snakes. Tell her to go home," said Cecil.

"Who made you the boss?" I said fiercely. He looked away. "Come on, Winnie."

She climbed down very carefully, as if she was afraid of falling.

"What's that?" she asked, pointing to the potato chips.

Ed pushed the bag at her. "Here, you can have some," he said. His voice was gentle. He didn't seem to mind Winnie.

Cecil was busy with the sandwich I had given Rita. He handed it to Winnie. She took a big bite out of it, smiling radiantly, her small white teeth covered with tomatoes, bread and . . .

"What did you put in that?" I cried, grabbing the rest of the sandwich.

"Worms. Snake Girl loves worms." Cecil looked proud of himself.

Rita laughed.

Winnie's face turned white. She gagged. The nether ends of at least two worms were sliding off the sodden bread in my hand. Winnie leaned over and was sick. It wasn't nice having to see our lunch again that way. Winnie began to sob, a shrill, nasty sound in the leaden summer day.

Ed stood up and dragged his pole from the river. A tiny fish flopped on the end like a piece of bedraggled silver. He quickly unhooked it and flung it back into the water.

50

"Yuck," said Cecil.

"You creep!" I looked away from him. Rita did too.

"Come on, Winnie," said Ed, putting his hand under her elbow and dragging her up the bank. She was still holding the bag of chips.

"You are disgusting," I told Cecil. His face was red. Rita looked ill, but she stayed where she was.

"I'm sorry," Cecil stammered. "I thought it was funny."

"Where I come from, we wouldn't do something like that to a dog," I said. "You're scum."

"It doesn't matter. We told you not to bring her anyway," said Rita coldly.

I walked up close to her. I had to tip my face up, because Rita loomed over me. "Winnie's a person," I said.

"She's a snake, a Snake Girl, and she eats worms!" Rita laughed. She gave me a little push. "If you like her so much, you hang around with her. But don't expect to be friends with us. You must just love snakes."

I was shaking, but I marched up the bank and joined Winnie and Ed on the bridge. Winnie was retching again, so we couldn't go anywhere right away. The chip bag was a sodden mass, but Winnie held it tightly.

I stared down at the river. Cecil was looking up at us, but Rita was sitting on the rock again, casting her line as if nothing mattered. She faced the river. Winnie gasped.

"You better take her home," Ed said quietly. He opened his shirt and, using the corner, wiped sweat and vomit from Winnie's pale face. "Pearl won't want her down here." He gently pried the bag of chips from her hands.

"How can you touch that?" I asked, jerking my head away from him. "And how do you know what Pearl wants and doesn't want?"

"Everybody knows Pearl," Ed said, "and everybody knows Winnie."

"Let's go, Winnie." I started to pull her away from Ed, and she started to cry louder, just like a baby.

"Stop crying," I snapped. "Be quiet!"

"Take it easy, Ohio," Ed said. "Winnie, go home with Bryn—go on now. Go on." He pushed her toward me, unlatching her arm from his own arm and uncurling her fingers from his shirt.

She came, but she sobbed all the way home, and I started to worry. If we both got into trouble for being at the river, she could only blame herself. I didn't invite her. But what would I tell Pearl and my dad?

I did feel a little sorry for her. I guess I'd cry if anyone let me eat a worm sandwich.

"Winnie, Winnie, stop crying," I tried again, dancing out in front of her.

She looked at me through tangled hair.

"Pearl's going to be real angry with me," I told her. "She's going to be mad at you, too."

"Mean!" Winnie said.

"Yes, they were mean," I agreed.

Winnie wiped her whole face, starting from her chin and sweeping up to her hairline with the back of her hand. She stopped crying. She looked terrible, though, pale and dirty. She didn't smell very good either.

"I'll help you clean up," I offered.

"Okay."

When we got to the house, I wiped her down as best I could with a dish towel and some soap, using water from the big kettle on the back of the wood stove.

Supper was to be vegetables from the garden, bread and butter, apple preserves, tea, and the rest of the pie we'd started on at lunch. Winnie was all right until we started setting the table; then she began to gag and ran outside. Looking puzzled, Pearl followed her.

Here it comes, I thought grimly.

"Winnie doesn't seem to be feeling well," Pearl said, coming back a few minutes later. "I'm sending her to bed. You'll have to get things together yourself. Your father and I have a few more things to see to, so just ring the bell when you're ready for us."

Winnie, white and wet with sweat, was sliding past me to the hall.

"Did you tell?" I whispered.

Winnie shook her head carefully and kept on walking.

Good. I was safe.

"You say grace tonight," Pearl said when the three of us were at the table.

"I don't know any," I said.

She looked at me sharply.

The morning bell rang, and the teacher, Mrs. Fields, came to the door. She was a tall, round woman with brown eyes and soft brown hair.

"Line up!" she called, and bodies of all shapes and sizes crowded toward the door.

"Good morning, boys and girls," she said.

"Good morning, Mrs. Fields."

"When I tap your shoulder, go into the second line, please," she said. She walked down the row tapping the smallest children lightly. They broke like startled rabbits and began to form another row beside us. Winnie was at the very back of the line. I twisted around to see what would happen.

"Hello, Winnie," Mrs. Fields said.

Winnie nodded. She was staring at her feet.

Mrs. Fields hesitated. "I think it's time you came into the big room, don't you?"

"Yes!" Winnie said. She looked so happy.

The talking started right away.

"Oh, no, not in our room!"

"Yech! Snakes in school!"

"Ooh, the Snake Girl is in with us."

Someone made a booing sound.

Winnie's expression melted, and she stared at her new shoes again.

Mrs. Fields looked around. All heads snapped forward to face the school building—all except mine. I was still facing the back of the line.

"Surely *you* didn't say anything, young lady?" Mrs. Fields asked. She sounded dangerous.

56

"No, ma'am."

"Turn around, then, please," she said.

It was the smallest school I've ever seen. Six windows lined one wall. Shelves of books lined the other—tattered books, books without covers, books with stains and rips on the outside, and, tucked among them, the occasional shining cover of a new book. Treasure. Even if I didn't make any friends, I could read for the rest of the year.

There were only four desks in each row, and only four rows. Mine was closest to the windows and farthest from the books. Winnie's was right behind me. She scraped her feet nervously against the back of my chair.

Mrs. Fields had a piano at the front of the room, a huge map of the world pulled down over the blackboard, and a great big desk with a bunch of purple asters in a jar sitting on it. Mrs. Fields opened the palms of her hands, wiggling her fingers. Everyone stood up and began to sing.

" 'Oh, Canada, our home and native land . . .' " Of course, I didn't know the words, so I just stood there. At home we said the Pledge of Allegiance. Here they said a prayer. " 'Our Father, who art in heaven . . .' " they began.

"Welcome back," Mrs. Fields said, when everyone was sitting down again. "Let's introduce ourselves to the new girl and have her tell us something about herself. She comes from the United States. Her name is Bryn, Bryn Cameron. Bryn?"

She wanted me to start talking? She'd already said everything they needed to know. I sat frozen at my desk, feeling my tongue swell and my face heat up. I was sick of school already.

"Bryn?"

"I, ah, I, er . . ."

"Bryn, in this school we stand up when we are speaking," Mrs. Fields prompted me.

I stared at her. I slid from my desk and leaned on it with one hand. My other hand found a place to hide in my stiff new skirt. I felt like a giant.

"I . . . I'm in sixth grade."

"No kidding?" someone said. There was a ripple of laughter, low, like wind.

"Yes . . ." Mrs. Fields pushed.

"I . . . used to live in a place called Circleville."

"Round town," somebody said. Was it Rita?

"It's in Ohio. It's the pumpkin capital of the world." Was I shouting? The tiny room now seemed very large, the sixteen students suddenly an ocean of faces. I couldn't really see them, though. Mrs. Fields was a white blur at the front of the room. I felt like I was going blind. How long did I have to talk?

I heard a sound then, a low, moaning sound. It was Winnie. I turned to look at her. The white terror on her face hit me like a slap. Her eyes were huge. She was more frightened than I was. Somehow, knowing that made me feel braver.

"We have a big celebration in my town, called Pumpkin Show," I told them. "People come from all over the country to see it, and we get out of school for three days. My father raised and trained horses for a man. We moved here this summer. I don't know how long we're staying.

"Not very long, I hope," I added softly, sitting down. Mrs. Fields was pointing to the world map.

"This is where Bryn comes from," she told the class. "Our first assignment will be to draw a map of Ohio and learn the different products that come from a place very similar in terrain to our own province of Ontario."

I looked around. I could see again. Ed was over near the bookcase, looking at me from under his fine white hair. His expression did not change, but he raised one hand and waved it slowly, close to the top of his desk.

Mrs. Fields took the roll call, and each student stood up to answer. The other kids all seemed to know one another. Cecil fired off a few rubber bands, but Mrs. Fields just went down and held out her hand, and he gave the rest to her. She kept on talking.

Winnie was the last one to be called. She rose, shaking, from her desk and squeaked, "Winnie. I'm Winnie." Her hands were twisted together.

"Do you want to tell us anything about your summer?" Mrs. Fields asked, but Winnie shook her head. I thought I knew why she said her name out loud again. She meant her name was not Snake Girl.

"I just want to let all of you know, as I do every year," Mrs. Fields said, "I expect you to treat one another with respect." Her eyes made a lighthouse beam around the classroom.

Drawing Ohio was easy for me. It seemed so far-away now. I felt dizzy. Here I was in a new school, in a new country, surrounded by new people. Even though I had lived in Circleville all my life, there was no one I knew left there. In a way I didn't really belong anywhere. I drew a picture of myself outside the lines of the map, floating.

The rest of the morning went by in a storm of paper, books, and map drawing. The pencil sharpener ground out a steady tune. Winnie was supposed to be in grade five, but she stayed sitting behind me anyway. Cecil and two other boys were in grade six with me and were moved near my desk. Ed was in seventh grade, Rita in eighth.

At lunchtime I grabbed the brown paper bag Pearl had given me and headed for the trees, looking for a place to hide. I climbed an old pine. Bits of needle got stuck in my hair. I ate my peanut butter and jelly sandwich up there, the same lunch I always had at the High Street School at home. I could hear kids playing softball and other kids singing skipping songs. I wondered how Winnie was doing, but I didn't leave the tree until the bell rang again. If I wasn't going to have any friends, I certainly wasn't going to stand around advertising the fact.

Mrs. Fields read to us before we did science. She promised she would read every day. My teacher last year never read to us. Mrs. Fields also gave us music lessons. She thumped out tunes on the piano, stopping to talk about note reading and lyrics, pauses and breaths. I raced through some math problems after that and found myself sitting, with nothing to do, looking out the window.

One of my troubles in school is that I finish my work so fast. I end up sitting, sitting, sitting. It looked like I was going to sit for another year.

Mrs. Fields cleared her throat. She was standing at my shoulder. "Bryn, you might try to take more care with your writing," she said, pointing to my scrawl. "It's pretty messy."

"Yes, ma'am." I was miserable.

Cecil turned around and made a face at me.

"Mr. Barton," Mrs. Fields said, but she didn't even look up at him. "Bryn, once your work is finished, you are welcome to go to the bookshelf and choose something to read. No point in just sitting, eh?"

"No, ma'am," I said, pleased to my bones. I looked over my writing, crossed a few *t*'s, then drifted over to the bookshelf and started browsing. Old magazines, lots of poetry, novels with strange titles. I found a book that looked interesting, and before I knew it the classroom had melted away.

Someone tripped over me and landed on the floor beside me. Rita.

"You stupid!" she shouted. Kids were laughing.

"Rita, Rita!" Mrs. Fields hurried over. "Are you hurt?"

"Yes." She stood up, scowling.

"There's no need for that tone. Sit down, please, dear. Bryn, read over in the window seat next time, please, or at your desk. Everyone, it's time for dismissal. And don't forget homework!"

We flew out the door, heading for home. It was a race, really, between Winnie and me, to see who would get away first. Her long legs carried her over the bridge and up the hill to the general store a lot faster than mine. I reached her, puffing, just as she started down our road.

We said nothing to each other, but the silence was friendly. We threw our books on Pearl's kitchen table and looked at the big plate of cookies waiting there. Winnie stuffed two into her mouth at once and began to chew. I gulped down one at a time. Chocolate rimmed Winnie's mouth. She pulled the milk out of the fridge, and I poured it into teacups. We drank like wolves.

"Well, you're in the big room," I said at last. I began to laugh, and she did, too. We tried to do some homework before Pearl came in, but only mine got finished. Winnie could hardly read a thing. Pearl spent a long time after supper helping her finish it.

Pearl never did say, but I can guess the difference between a group home and Pearl's house. Pearl makes cookies and she knows who is going to eat them. Pearl will help with the same thing over and over again without getting impatient. She is someone who can wait and wait and wait for you to learn something, no

62

matter how long it's going to take. Pearl loves Winnie, and Winnie loves Pearl. I hadn't been with them very long, but it was hard to imagine the two of them anywhere but in this house, and together.

9

"THAT you, Bryn?" When I came down for breakfast on Saturday, Dad was sitting at the table with a paper napkin covering his face. He had a pair of Pearl's reading glasses stuck over the napkin, which blew out gently from where it hid his mouth. He looked like an intelligent ghost.

It's so strange about him. For a month he just floated between the barn and his room, stopping only for meals in the kitchen, giving me an occasional hug. He looked cheerful as he went about his work, but he hardly spoke at all. And he never spoke about what would happen next.

Now, here he was, in disguise. He hadn't goofed around like that since way before Mom died. They used to playact with each other, talk in silly voices. And I remember him coming in one night from Mr. Trenton's barn with two dandelions stuck in his ears. He didn't say anything about them, just let the flowers wag away till we sat down to eat. It's like there's this other Dad inside him, but that one only comes out sneakily, when I'm not looking.

"Yes," I said, smiling now. "Is that you, Dad?"

"Could be." He swept the glasses and napkin from his face and stood up. "Want to look at Pearl's farm later this morning? I have a few more chores to do in the barn, but then we could go exploring."

"Great!" I said. "I'll be right here." I couldn't stop smiling as I scooped up a cold piece of toast, a glass of milk, and a book. Dad finally had some time for me! I took myself out to the big tree near the porch. Pearl was painting the bottom latticework. She put down her brush.

"Bryn . . ." she began. Reluctantly, I put the book on the grass.

"What do you want me to do, Pearl? Dad's taking me for a walk, so I better get my work out of the way."

Surprisingly, she said, "No, not work. I thought we could talk."

"Well, okay," I said. What a morning! "What do you want to talk about?"

"I told you, I'm not good at this," Pearl said gruffly, picking up her paintbrush and looking more like her usual self. "You choose."

"Will you tell me about Winnie's father?" I'd been wanting to know. But I wondered if I'd started out too strong. There was a long pause.

"What about Earl?" Pearl looked sour. She jammed the paintbrush into the can and turned around to look at me. And then, most surprising of all, she smiled, really smiled and came over to sit beside me.

"Earl was wonderful. I miss him."

"What happened?"

"He died a long time ago," she said. "When Winnie was still a little girl. It was his heart. He wasn't young—we weren't young—when Winnie was born."

She rubbed her eyes. "He was a good man, but he wouldn't sit down, not even when he was exhausted. I guess you could say he worked himself to death on this old farm."

Pearl worked harder than anyone I'd ever met. It was hard to imagine Earl working any harder.

"That's sad," I said.

"Sure, it's sad. Life has sad parts to it," Pearl said. "Luckily, there's lots of happy parts, too, and Earl was one of the best parts of my life." She smiled again at me. "I've often thought that when a family loses one good heart, it has to grow a new one. He left me this farm and he gave me Winnie. Sometimes I feel he's still here with us." She wiped her face with the corner of her work shirt.

"I don't mean he's really here," she added, looking at me. "It's just that I still have good, strong memories of him, so many of them that I still know him very well." She took my hand roughly and squeezed it.

"What would he have done about people who are mean to Winnie?" I asked cautiously.

Her mood changed. "What sort of people?" she asked crisply.

"Oh, you know. Like Rita Pisgah."

Pearl's tone softened. "Oh, Rita. Rita has her own problems."

"Rita?" Big Rita?

66

"Sure," Pearl said easily. "She's not a very happy girl."

I wanted to ask more, but Pearl seemed to be finished with Rita. She got up to go back to her painting.

"Wait, can I ask you one more thing?"

"Is this talking?" Pearl asked, but there was still a smile on her face. "Seems more like plain gossip to me."

"I have a lot of catching up to do," I answered. "Don't forget, I haven't lived here all my life. There are lots of things I don't know."

"True," Pearl said. "Fire away."

"Cecil's dad . . . what happened to him?"

"Drank himself to death," Pearl said bluntly.

"But that's terrible."

"Yes." She shot me a clear, level look.

"It's not true about kids' lives being perfectly happy, is it?" I said, more to myself than to Pearl.

"You thought you were the only one?" Pearl asked, just as softly. She had begun painting rapidly.

"Yes," I said to my book. I picked it up and began to read. When I looked up again, Pearl was gone. The new paint shone, still wet. Dad was coming up the path from the barn.

"Let's grab some sandwiches," he said.

We walked over a makeshift bridge across the river to the grove of trees I could see from my bedroom window. The air was as clean as Pearl's sheets. My dad was ahead of me.

"Look," he said, pointing to a small building with one dirty window. "Pearl has a sugar shed."

"What's that?"

"It's a place to cook up the sap collected from these trees in the early spring. We can build a huge fire in there and boil the runoff until it's maple syrup."

I love sweet things. Having our own supply of maple syrup sounded good to me. And he'd said spring. Did that mean we would still be here? I so much wanted to ask, but I was afraid. Did I *want* to be here? If we weren't, if we'd moved on, where would we be then?

An old tombstone tilted from the crest of a small hill up ahead. My father stopped there, his hands loose by his sides. He sat down. "Come here," he said. He patted the ground beside him.

We sat there for a long time, my dad's face all quiet and tipped up to the sky. I read the inscription on the stone.

Here lies my Margaret Pearl
and our infant daughter.
Taken May 31, 1880.
May they rest in peace.

I wondered who they were. I could imagine a sad husband laying a gravestone and walking away through the woods, leaving his wife and baby behind him. It seemed a lonely place to leave your family even though the sun shone through the thick leaves, scattering light across the earth around us.

Birds and squirrels whispered overhead, sounds of

a secret life. My dad struck a wooden match against a rock and lit a cigarette. He put his arm around me, and I leaned against his shoulder. I began to feel sleepy.

"Falcons," my dad said suddenly, his finger tracing their flight. There were two of them, spiraling lazily down over Pearl's field.

I sat up. My chest hurt in an odd way. I felt as if I'd scraped myself. I rubbed the places where it chafed. Two little cones had grown on my normally very flat chest. They felt like tiny volcanoes without pointed tops. I looked down and pulled my T-shirt tight. I was growing breasts. When did it happen?

I was so surprised I snorted, and my father looked over at me. I felt my face grow warm with embarrassment. I let my shirt fly loose instantly.

Dad stared. He looked startled. "You'll have to talk to Pearl, my girl," he said. Silence. "There are some things I can't help you with," he continued hesitantly. "You can take your questions to her. She's a good soul."

I had forgotten, or maybe never really believed, that I would be a woman someday. Here I was crouched in a bunch of trees, and it hit me. How could I not have noticed what was happening?

I wished fiercely that Mom could be here. She would have laughed and told me what I wanted to know even before I thought to ask her.

"Dad," I said. "Dad."

"What, honey?" He unfolded himself from the ground and stood up.

"Wait," I said. I held my hands out, and he pulled

69

me up, too, but then he let go and moved away. I didn't want him to fly off into the trees.

"Dad, you said 'spring' back there by that shed. Are we going to stay here?" I asked him.

"I don't know," he said slowly. "I can't decide."

I felt suddenly urgent. "If you can't decide, I can't decide either, right? If you don't stay, I don't stay. Why should I talk to Pearl if we're leaving?"

"You make your home where you are," Dad said slowly, thinking about it. He was looking at me as if he didn't know me.

"Is that true, Dad?" I asked, raising my voice. "Being in the truck with you on the way up here wasn't being home. Ohio now wouldn't be home."

My father winced, but he didn't answer me.

"I want to be home, somewhere," I said breathlessly. "I want something to be my place."

My father nodded, but he looked dazed.

"Please, Dad," I said, holding my hands out again and walking over to him. "Let's stay here. I want to stay. Maybe I could help you out more in the barn?"

He frowned, and I felt like crying.

"I'm lonely," I whispered. "I want you to talk to me more, Dad. I miss . . . I miss *you*."

"But I'm right here."

"We don't talk, though. We don't do things together. Sometimes it's as if you've gone away, like Mom. . . ."

"But I am here," he said. "Right here." He tried a smile. "Come on."

70

Walking with him the rest of the afternoon, I watched warily. He didn't move on ahead, but stayed by my side, silent. I might have been one kind of animal watching another. He was still the father I knew, but he was somebody else, too, somebody separate from me, not just my dad. I was afraid of becoming somebody separate.

10

DAD didn't need help with the milking, but I hung around the barn while he was finishing his chores and fed carrots from the garden to Ginger, Snap, and Bauble. We walked back to the house together. He smiled faintly at me as we climbed the porch steps, and pulled a piece of straw from my hair.

The mood changed as soon as we got inside the door. Maybe it was all the talking that they'd done that afternoon. Who knows? Maybe it strained Pearl and Dad because, like that, they seemed to be spoiling for a fight.

"Go ahead and wash up, David," Pearl said before Dad had even taken off his work hat.

"Certainly, ma'am," my father said. Unsmiling now, he went to the sink and washed his arms, hands, face, and neck with Pearl's harsh, white soap. He made a big production of it, scrubbing and scrubbing until bubbles flew from his skin. As Pearl put the platter of ham on the table, he dried himself with the rough towel. He sat down then, staring at his plate.

72

Winnie, Pearl, and I were waiting, but no one spoke. Pearl cleared her throat. I saw color rising in her face. Winnie reached for the platter, and Pearl smacked her fingers sharply. Winnie's face twisted for a moment, but she took a look at Pearl and decided not to cry. My father didn't raise his eyes.

"David!" Pearl's voice was sharp. "Will you please say grace?"

My father's head snapped up. He looked very, very angry.

"I think I told you we didn't say grace at home," he said. "Does living with you require that we do everything your way?" His voice was shaking.

"It's just common courtesy," Pearl shot back. "Why do you have such a problem with a simple prayer?"

Winnie and I were pinned to that table like moths.

"Common courtesy," repeated my father. "I'm trying to be as courteous as I know how. You sit there blaming me every single day for your sister's death. I know I should have helped her to come back into the family. I know I should have seen how ill she was. Maybe she didn't have to die. Isn't that what you're thinking?"

His voice stumbled and tripped and rose again. "Don't you think I am punished enough without seeing the blame on your face every single day?"

"I blame you?" Pearl's eyes were full of tears that did not fall. "I blame myself. I was her sister. I felt I had to choose between Winnie and her, and I chose Winnie, didn't I?"

Pearl stood up. Her back was straight as a wall, but her hands trembled even though she held them tightly in front of her. My plate shone up at me, empty except for the faint pale reflection of my own face. I tried to imagine my mother in this room, in this house. Just then, I could hardly remember what my mother looked like.

"Why didn't she tell me she was ill? Why didn't she tell me?" Now tears did spill down Pearl's face.

"Is it too painful to have us here? Have I done the right thing?" My father seemed to be talking to himself. They both were. They talked over each other.

"I lost her years ago," Pearl said, "but now, with Bryn here, it's like having her and not having her, all over again. I want to make it right, and Julia didn't give me a chance."

"Maybe I shouldn't have come. I just didn't know where else to go, what to do," my father murmured.

"I'm glad you came, can't you get that through your fool head!" Pearl shouted. "It takes time for people to learn to live together, but we can do it. We can do this. For heaven's sake, David, give me a chance."

"I'm sorry, Pearl, I'm sorry," my father mumbled. Pearl left the table and he followed her.

The second they were out the kitchen door, Winnie pulled the platter to her and scooped up a big slice of ham. She took bites out of it while dipping into the cooling boiled potatoes with her other hand. A bite of potato, a bite of ham, and big gulps of milk from her glass. Winnie was eating supper all by herself. Winnie was destroying supper. Food gathered in greasy

74

streaks around her mouth and clotted her hair. She wiped her hands across the front of her dress. Her eyes were clear and empty.

At that moment, I saw that we were all separate.

That night, I couldn't sleep. Every time I closed my eyes, I started to think about Mom. I didn't want to think about her.

It was cold, and I wrapped my quilt around my shoulders and stared out the window. I tried not to think about anything at all. Anytime a thought circled in and tried to dive through the wall of my heart, I just stiffened my body and made my gaze harder. Thoughts bounced off me like dead flies.

I saw my dad come back from the barn. I heard Pearl go in to Winnie, then to her own room. Much later, I heard my dad come upstairs. I didn't move. Maybe I even slept, sitting up, for a while.

When the moon was high over the barn, I crept downstairs and filled a teacup with milk. I sat at the table. It was still warm in the kitchen. My book of poems was sitting on a chair nearby, and I reached for it. There was a pen sitting on it, and when I lifted the poems I spied a tuft of paper beneath the book. It was a letter my dad must have been writing. I knew I shouldn't look at it, but I did. When I saw who it was for, I was frightened.

"Dear Julia," it began. I read it anyway.

I feel you would want to know how Bryn is doing. We haven't been in Canada long, but our girl is settling

75

in bravely enough. She seems to have made some friends and she chips in when there's work to be done. There's always work to be done, isn't there, Julia, no matter what?

Pearl is good to us. She's taken us in with no question at all, though she was mighty surprised to learn we had a daughter.

Pearl is still the same as I remember her—tough as old beef on the outside, but kinder, very gentle behind those snappy eyes. That she dotes on her daughter is plain enough to me, but she's strict with the girl. Winnie's a pleasant little thing, odd looking but affectionate. I know Pearl wants to like our Bryn. She hasn't quite decided what to make of her.

I can't decide either, Julia. Bryn isn't happy. She's not always kind to Winnie. Pearl and I are watchful, but it's hard to know just what to do or what to say. You know, I've never been one to find such things easy.

Bryn's grieving over you, Julia. She's too serious. She's always watching me, as if she thinks I can bring you back somehow. Sometimes I think she believes I *can* bring you back and am just too mean to do it. I always miss you for myself, but today I miss you, especially hard, for Bryn. I wish you could come to her and talk like you used to do. She's up in her room. I can feel how alone she is—how alone we both are, without you. I don't even know what to ask her. You were always the one to handle the tough stuff.

I thought maybe by writing this down, it would seem as if you and I were working this thing out for our girl, planning what we might do, together, to make it right.

And now I've done it, I have nowhere to send this

letter, Julia. I guess the truth is that from now on, I'm going to have to handle the tough stuff by myself. I'm not good at it. You were always my teacher.

I am still your loving husband, David.

All the waiting thoughts rose up and rushed in on me, and I began to cry.

DREAM

I AM AT THE EDGE OF THE CORNFIELD, staring into the pasture. Only the horses are there, grazing under a cloudy sky.

"There's something I want to tell you," I say, but I am puzzled. I can't remember what it is. An idea is trying to push into my thoughts, but it keeps slipping away from me.

"Mom?"

But she's not there. I know she isn't coming, but I stand a long time in the corn, waiting.

11

ED turned out to be really smart. He sat at the back of the classroom with his long legs stretched from beneath his desk. He usually looked as if he were sleeping or about to melt away.

He would cross his arms and keep his head down, but any time I looked over his eyes were bright under the flop of white hair. He watched everything and everyone.

"Who knows the capital of England?" Mrs. Fields might ask.

During the pause that followed, everyone in the room would look at Ed. Even Mrs. Fields. Another moment, then Ed would pull himself up out of his odd arrangement, sit straight, raise only the palm of his hand from the desk, and wait.

"Ed?"

"London." He always spoke politely.

"What is a descriptive word called?"

Silence.

"Ed?"

"An adjective."

"Would someone please name the parts of an insect's life cycle?"

Silence.

"Ed?"

And so it went.

There were times when Mrs. Fields ignored his long white fingers as they rose from the desk.

"Rita?"

"Bill?"

"Henry?"

"Jessica?"

"Bryn?"

And we would shuffle up an answer if we could, or stammer an excuse if we could not.

Other times Ed was the one who fell back. When she asked the kind of question that hung in the air, he turned his head to look out the window. He didn't raise his hand. Sometimes, she asked him anyway, and then he would answer. Sometimes she'd just leave him alone. Maybe it's hard to be that smart.

Ed sure seemed shy. Rita called him Egghead and Brains. He didn't seem to mind.

There were at least two things I liked about Ed. He loved books and never tried to hide his interest in them. He spent lots of his free time at the bookshelf, just like I did, and he always took books home at night to read.

The other thing I liked was his voice. It was beautiful, rich and husky. When he talked, his words were slices of sound, crisp at the edges and deep in the middle. I tried to make him talk just so I could listen to him.

"Ed, what's this one about?" I would ask him, waving a book I had pulled off the shelf.

"Look again, Ohio," he said one time. "That's the dictionary."

"Want to ride bikes tomorrow?" I asked him one Friday after school. We were walking home.

"Sorry, Ohio, I can't," he answered. "Maybe some other time."

Catch me asking him again. I wouldn't have the courage. I shrugged and said, "Sure."

Cecil liked to ride his bike without using his hands. Sometimes you could see him using his knees a little to keep the handlebars on course, but most of the time he cruised lazily up and down the main street with knees pumping slowly, arms crossed over his chest.

One afternoon he was practicing circles in front of the general store when Winnie and I came up to get some cheese for Pearl. It had been raining hard all day, and the ditches along the road were soft and muddy. Cecil waved.

"Come on, Winnie," I said to her, but she stopped and looked at Cecil admiringly. I guess Winnie wasn't the grudge-bearing type.

"See?" she asked me, pointing. Then she gave one of her rich belly laughs.

"Hey, girls," Cecil called, deep in the middle of his next circle. "Watch this!" and he raised his hands high over his head. Knees pumping furiously, hands high, Cecil sped toward us. Winnie and I stepped aside, but Cecil—Cecil "No Hands"—had turned and was heading straight for Rachel and Virginia's house.

"Whee-ha!" he screamed, and then he lost control of the bike. It happened so fast he didn't have time to stop smiling. He flew gracefully over the top of the handlebars and slid, face first, down the length of a mud-filled ditch. Winnie and I hadn't moved before Cecil leaped up again. His entire face was covered in slick, black mud. His hair had disappeared under a tight cap of it. Suddenly he opened his eyes, and those blues, shining at us like marbles, made us start laughing. Cecil's mouth opened, and that looked even more strange. He was a mud boy with real eyes, real mouth. He started crying and ran for home, leaving the bike perched like a broken eagle on the edge of the road.

Winnie and I laughed helplessly. Tears squirted out of Winnie's eyes, and my nose was running. For a moment there I thought I was going to wet myself.

We went in to get the cheese. Pearl liked to buy a huge round of it. The grocer cut it in half and wrapped each half wheel separately in brown paper. Even so, the pieces were heavy. When we came out, Cecil was back, bending over his bike with a scowl. Most of the mud had been rinsed out of his hair and from his face, but his ears were still filled with dirt and his clothes were black.

Winnie said, "Whee-ha!" in my ear, and we laughed all over again.

82

"Just help me get this bicycle chain back on," Cecil muttered.

We put the cheese halves down in the road. I kept the handlebars straight, and Winnie held the back wheel while Cecil wrestled with the chain. I thought we would be only a moment.

"Don't mess with my bike—just hold it," he said, sprinting away. "I've got to get a little oil."

"Bryn!" Winnie whispered. "Ouch! Bryn!"

"What is it?" It was starting to rain again.

Winnie had jammed her finger in the bicycle chain. She must have poked it in. Tears started streaming down her cheeks.

"Oh, Winnie!"

"Ouch! Ouch!" she whispered, chest heaving. She tried to scramble away from the chain on her knees, but her finger was firmly pinched. The whole bike started to drag after her.

"Gee, Winnie!" cried Cecil, who had reappeared with the oil. "Why did you do that?" He smeared some of the oil on her stuck finger.

"It's gonna hurt for a minute," he told her. He tugged on her palm until the finger popped out. She plunged her greasy hand into her pocket, sniffling.

"Sorry, sorry," she whispered. She wiped her eyes with her other arm.

"Why are you whispering?" I asked her.

"Don't mess with bike," she said, looking meekly at the bicycle chain.

Cecil laughed.

"Whee-ha!" Winnie tried, rather boldly, beginning to smile.

Cecil laughed even louder. We headed back to Pearl's.

We only remembered the cheese when we were nearly home. We ran back to get it, but someone had driven over the halves, and we found only squashed paper with orange blobs hanging out the sides. We figured Pearl wouldn't want to see her cheese in that condition, so we unwrapped it and threw it into the river. The water was high from the rain, and the cheese bounced on the surface only once before vanishing. I don't know why we didn't think to get rid of the paper.

"Oh, oh, trouble," Winnie said.

"Yeah."

And there was.

"Well, where's the cheese?" Pearl demanded, taking the clumps of wet, muddy paper from my hands.

Winnie looked terrified.

"Where's the cheese, Winnie?" Pearl repeated.

"Lost it!" Winnie said.

"You lost it?" Pearl smoothed the ruined paper against her apron, where it made a splotch. "A great big girl like you! You get up to your room and stay there, miss, until I call you down."

Winnie began crying noisily and stomped upstairs.

"I suppose you were with her?" Pearl said, almost sweetly.

I watched her carefully. "Sure. You sent both of us."

"And together you both managed to lose pounds and pounds of cheese," Pearl said, still sweetly. "I do emphasize the amount . . . really *pounds* of cheese."

"Uh, yeah," I stammered.

I looked down the same time Pearl did, and we both saw the big tire mark on the paper. Pearl's head snapped up. I headed for the hallway. I figured I'd be sent to my room anyway and might as well get a head start. I heard a strange, rasping sound, like sand scraping on glass. I turned and saw that Pearl . . . Pearl was laughing. She held the crushed paper to her breast, leaning against the wall. She poked her finger upward, nodding at me, still laughing.

"You want me to get Winnie?"

She nodded, laughing.

I ran up the steps three at a time to Winnie's room. I knocked. Tears were still wet on her cheeks.

"Come down, Winnie," I said. "It's okay. She knows."

Winnie looked at me.

"Come on, she knows and it's okay," I repeated.

Winnie took my hand and came down.

Pearl was wiping her eyes on the apron. "I suppose," she said, "you were together when the car hit that cheese?"

"We didn't even see the car," I said honestly.

"Thank God you weren't under those tires," said Pearl. It was hard to tell from her voice if she was laughing or crying, but she grabbed Winnie's face with both her hands and kissed her loudly on the forehead.

Then she smacked her lightly on the bottom and pushed her toward the door.

"Put on your raincoats," she said, "and you think twice before you tell me a lie again, young ladies." She was laughing again and she gave me a smack on the bottom and a push toward the door as well. "I'll make supper. Skeddaddle."

I couldn't believe it. Pearl actually had a sense of humor.

We still had more than an hour until the evening meal, but it was starting to get dark and the rain was coming down harder.

"Barn?" Winnie asked brightly.

"Let's walk in the rain," I said.

"Cold." Winnie headed for the barn.

"Okay. I'll be there in a minute," I called after her. I tramped up the road toward the general store, listening to the mud squelch under my boots.

"Boo," Cecil shouted in my ear. I almost hit him, I was so startled. He was still in the same filthy clothes and by now soaking wet. I didn't see any bike.

"What are you doing out?" I asked.

"Just horsing around," he said. "What are you doing? And where's the Snake Girl?"

"Don't call her that," I said. "Her name is Winnie."

"Yeah. Well, what do you do down there?" he asked, waving at Pearl's farm.

"Oh, just horse around." I grinned. "Work, mostly. Pearl always has us doing something."

"Yeah. Leila always wants me to do something,

too," Cecil said. He fell into step beside me. He started singing "I Wanna Hold Your Hand," and then he started talking about hockey.

"Cecil, don't you like Leila?" I asked.

"Sure. She's okay," he said.

"You're not very nice to her."

"How do you know?" he asked, staring at me.

I shrugged.

"She's not my real mother, you know. But I do a lot of work to help out at home. That's really why I work at the store."

"She's beautiful."

"Aw, so what," he said. "So is baby Frances, my sister. But never mind about them. Come over here. I want to show you something." He stood under a tree with his hands in his pockets. "Come *on!*"

"We better go soon," I said, walking closer.

Cecil grabbed me and shoved his lips all over my nose, then pressed his mouth, hard, on mine. His breath smelled like tuna fish.

"Cecil!" I pushed him away and wiped my face on my sleeve. "Don't you ever do that to me again!"

"What'll you do about it?" He smirked.

I considered. "I'll think of something you'll hate," I said. "Believe it."

"Aw, Bryn . . ."

"I mean it. That's disgusting."

"Sorry."

His face was very red. He offered me some bubble gum from a package of damp baseball cards he had in his pocket. I took some. He walked back down the road to Pearl's with me.

Winnie was setting the table for Pearl when I got in. Pearl had actually made tuna casserole. Winnie offered me a spoonful when Pearl went out to get wood for the stove.

"No, thanks," I said. "You eat it." I could hear Pearl cleaning her boots on the porch.

"Winnie," I said softly.

"Yes?"

"Cecil kissed me."

Winnie looked at me quietly. Without smiling, she whispered back, "Whee-ha!" and we both laughed. Then:

"You like kissing?" she asked.

"Yuck."

"A boy didn't kiss me," she said.

"Maybe one will, someday," I said importantly. Then, more honestly, I added, "It's not that much fun, anyway."

"Not fun," she echoed. She looked puzzled.

Pearl bustled through the door in her work socks, carrying some wood. "Getting chilly," she said cheerfully.

88

12

I HAD a postcard of the Circleville Pumpkin Show. It showed the grand tier of pumpkins, starting with five-hundred-pound gourds at the base and climbing into a tall pyramid with one tiny round pumpkin at the top. Until I started showing it around, nobody believed what I said about the size of those pumpkins.

"When is this show, Ohio?" Ed asked me.

"They usually have it the third week in October," I told him. "Look, here's one of the seeds I got from Mr. Trenton. He grows pumpkins every year for the competition."

"It looks like one from 'Jack and the Magic Beanstalk,'" Ed said, holding the thumb-sized seed in the palm of his hand.

"Aw, how do they grow pumpkins that big?" Rita said, grabbing the seed.

"The farmers keep their growing tricks a secret. I've heard some of them go out and sing to their pumpkins. Others feed them milk."

"Milk?" Rachel was sitting beside Rita.

She had come into our room for lunch. The teachers were eating in the other room. It had been raining hard for days. The whole school felt dark and damp. Kids were pretty well scattered and doing what they wanted, sitting on their desks reading, eating, or playing with board games.

Rita started to laugh. "How can a pumpkin drink milk?"

"I'm not sure," I admitted. "Maybe they stick it in with needles."

"That's stupid," said Rita.

"I don't know," Ed said. "For sure they'd need a lot of water. Why not milk?"

"They have a parade in Circleville every day of the show, and the kids get out of school on Wednesday so they can celebrate the rest of the week," I told them.

"Whew, I'd like that part," said Rita, trying to wipe Rachel's face with the hem of her skirt.

"I can do it," Rachel said irritably. "I'm not a baby." She picked up Rita's hem and daintily wiped her mouth with it.

Virginia was sitting near the window with Winnie. They were looking at a picture book together and were sharing Pearl's chocolate chip cookies. I don't think Winnie had ever asked me about Circleville, just about my mom.

I told Ed and Rita about Little Miss Pumpkin, a small girl chosen every year to be the princess and to ride in the parades. I told them about the rides, the food, the exhibits of flowers, vegetables, quilts, and artwork.

90

"Sounds just like the Metcalfe Fair," Rita said scornfully.

"I bet it's a lot bigger," I said. "People come to Pumpkin Show from all over the country. I can't imagine people coming from all over Canada to go to Metcalfe."

Rita shrugged and finished up the rest of Rachel's chocolate cupcake. "Looks like you're going to miss your pumpkin deal this year."

"Where's my seed?" I asked, annoyed.

"I ate it," she said, giving me a push. "You're always putting on airs."

"Now you'll really grow into a giant," Rachel said anxiously, looking up at Rita as if she expected her to shoot up into the sky.

"Rita Pisgah!" I shouted. "You're meaner than a wild pig." I yanked her hair, hard, and she slapped me.

"I don't care what you think," she huffed, but there were tears in her eyes. "You're just a stupid pumpkinhead from the south and you don't know anything."

Ed sighed and led Rachel toward the door. It was time for her and Virginia to head back to their own classroom, anyway. Mrs. Fields was coming in, but I got in a good pinch before she reached the desk. Rita's face was crimson, and her eyes had gone all small.

"Rita, you'll empty the trash cans after school for fighting," Mrs. Fields said. I stuck out my tongue. "And Bryn, you'll write a letter to your father, explaining what happened, and bring it back to me tomorrow with his signature. That's it, girls. To your seats, please."

"But she—" I started.

"I don't want to hear it, Bryn," Mrs. Fields snapped. "You're too old to be fighting like that. It's pure foolishness. There are other ways to work out your differences. Talking things through would be an excellent start. I don't want to see you fighting again, here or anywhere."

My punishment was worse than Rita's. It wasn't fair. Her parents wouldn't even know what happened. It takes only a few minutes to clean up trash.

Dear Dad,

 I was fighting with Rita Pisgah and got caught. We're not supposed to fight at school.

Your daughter,
Bryn

My dad read my letter and signed it. He didn't even look at me when he handed it back. He didn't seem to care who Rita was or anything. Of course, he'd hardly been into town, so how could he know her or how mean she was?

"Dad?"

"Yes?"

"Aren't you going to say anything?"

"There's nothing to say," he answered, and left the room. That hurt more than anything Mrs. Fields or Rita could dream up.

That night, Winnie brought Mike to my room. We

let him run around on the bed, but I was careful not to touch him myself. I didn't want to scare him—or Winnie.

It went on raining. The Metcalfe Fair was coming up the first week in October. We were making safety posters at school to enter in the accident prevention contest. The winners would be displayed Friday and Saturday when the fair was open to the public. My safety poster showed a red-haired girl standing in a puddle with an electric cord in her hand. The cord was plugged in to a wall outlet, and her hair was sticking up all over her head. The caption read "It's not safe to mix water and electricity." I made the eyes on the girl with big circles and green sparks flying out. Since Rita was the only red-haired girl in the school, most people could figure out who the girl in the picture was supposed to be.

Coming home from school Tuesday, with Winnie tagging along beside me, I saw Rita and Cecil on the bridge over the Castor River. Rachel and Virginia were peeking through the railing but holding firmly on to Rita's hands. When she saw me, Rita laughed and leaned over to whisper something in Cecil's ear. My skin burned.

"There she goes," Rita chanted. "Miss Know-it-all, Miss Pumpkin Pew!" She dug Cecil in the ribs with an elbow. He laughed nervously.

Without thinking, I climbed right up the rail of the

bridge and walked slowly forward, staring down at Rita. I knew I was up high where it was dangerous to be, but I just paid attention to putting one foot carefully in front of the other and kept focused on Rita's face. She went pale, and her mouth fell open.

"Bryn," she whispered, "come down."

"Why, am I scaring you?" I said, making my voice nasty. "Bet you can't do this, you coward."

I inched my foot forward again and moved closer to her. She looked flatter and smaller, somehow. I knew she wouldn't dare climb up behind me. I took another step, then stopped. I was suddenly aware of the sound of angry water boiling around the base of the bridge, and the whistle of the wind in my ears. Rita was whimpering, "Come down, come down," in a meek little voice.

I laughed. "You won't be calling me any more names, Miss Mushface," I told her. "You haven't even got the guts to climb up here with me."

Slowly, like a person under a spell, Rita dropped the twins' hands and moved toward me. She pulled herself up to the rail, but she just hung there, on her belly, clutching the slim steel rail, her feet waving safely near the ground. I turned around to face her, and she cringed.

Rachel was screaming and screaming. I looked down and saw the water of the Castor River, a swollen monster racing far below. And Virginia was down there, slipping into the current even as I watched her, her shiny patent leather shoes being swallowed. She must have been trying to get to the fishing rock, now covered by the flood.

Rita fell from the railing onto the road. Cecil was already scrambling down the bank, but I knew he wouldn't make it in time. Virginia looked up as the water took her. Her pale face was like a question to me across all that distance.

I guess I said my first real prayer before I jumped, and I was still praying when I fell toward the water. Like a hawk dropping for a mouse, I rushed through the air. I prayed there would be no rocks. I prayed the water would be deep enough to catch me. I prayed that I could reach Virginia. It was a fast prayer, and all I actually said was, "Please, God," for when I hit the water the cold smashed my breath away.

Virginia was already under water, her arms feeble stems above the current. I grabbed her braid as the water roared around us. It pulled us under the bridge. I tried to yank her closer to me, but the water pushed us apart, like the wrong ends of a magnet. I kicked and scrabbled, trying to find something to brace against or wrap my legs around. There was nothing. I fought harder. We were going too fast.

At home, in Ohio, the Island Road Quarry, in its deepest place, is always still. This water was alive with fury, a gobbling, crazy creature. It was taking me away, and I didn't want to go. I yelled, "No! No!"

Shouting helped. I pulled on Virginia's braid again, and her face turned up to the air. I got a grip on her shoulder. Now the water pushed her closer, and I tucked my arms beneath her armpits, crossing one arm over her chest. Her head went under again, and I reared back, pulling up. I could see her head again. Water streamed from her face.

"Bryn, grab it, grab it!" Cecil was on the bank, still downriver from me, holding out a slim trunk of wood. It looked too thin to hold a bird. I was still too far center, the water pulling me fast.

Kick, kick, I told myself, and my legs did what I told them. I pushed again. Virginia was limp in my arms. I'd have to let her go under once more to make it to the piece of wood.

"Grab it!" Cecil wailed.

Grab it, I told myself. Just grab it. I lunged for it, letting Virginia's face dip a third time into the water. I pushed again, holding her locked to my chest, and we rose, like some weird sea monster, from the water and clung to the thread of wood.

Cecil pulled us. He braced against our weight, gasping, dragging the limb backward. My feet found rocks, but water surged around me and I couldn't stand up. I couldn't help Cecil get us out.

He dropped the branch and snatched me, pulling me over the last few rocks on my side. He pulled and pulled, and at last I was out of the water. But I didn't let go of Virginia. She gagged. Her braid was still wrapped around my hand.

Then my father was there. He was trying to pry Virginia from my arms, but I was frozen to her. He pulled both of us into a standing position. My legs wobbled like a string puppet's. Virginia was a terrible weight, her hair an anchor chain I could not unravel.

"Let go, Bryn," he said.

"Don't, don't," I cried.

He smacked my face, his hand a fire on my cold cheek. Then I dropped her, dropped her as if she were trash, on the bank of the Castor River.

13

I CAN'T remember much about what happened at the river after I dumped Virginia on the ground. I know that Leila came and wrapped her in one of my father's gray horse blankets. Mrs. Fields turned up, somehow, and took everybody else away. My father drove me and Winnie home to Pearl.

Pearl bathed me herself, scrubbing my hair and skin until I cried in the hot soapy water that filled the old bathtub.

"You're hurting me!" I complained. "I can take a bath by myself."

"You're not going to catch your death with pneumonia," Pearl said, her mouth grim.

"Pearl!" I complained again, pushing her hands away.

"Hold still," Pearl shouted. She sounded so dangerous I didn't speak again until I was in the kitchen rocking chair, wearing one of her flannel nightgowns and wrapped in a quilt.

There were a lot of people there. Rita had come with

her mother. Mrs. Pisgah was a big woman with hair as red as her daughter's. She was weeping noisily into a large handkerchief.

Cecil and Leila were there. I watched Leila nurse Frances. Her face was peaceful as she held her baby, and when Frances went to sleep Leila snuggled the infant to one side of her lap and reached for Cecil with her free hand. Cecil left his hand in hers, but he stared only at the floor.

Dad sat near me on Pearl's work stool, and Pearl leaned against the sink, her arms protectively crossed over Winnie's chest. It looked as if Pearl were holding her hostage. The room was very quiet.

The Pulumbos were the last to arrive. When they came, Dr. Pulumbo looked like an entirely different person from the woman who had examined me in her office. Her hair was flattened down, and her glasses were gone. Her face was white as paper. Her husband, a rather fat man, kept his arm around her shoulders. Pearl brought them tea, which they accepted silently.

"We're here," said Pearl quietly, "to understand what happened this afternoon, and to make sure nothing like this ever"—she paused and looked over at me—"that nothing like this ever happens again," she finished.

"Virginia's fine," said Dr. Pulumbo, her voice wobbling. "She only swallowed a little water and she's badly bruised, but she'll be just fine. . . ." She began to cry softly. Her husband pulled her close again and fished around in his pocket for a handkerchief. He looked as if he might burst into tears himself.

"Their grandmother is home with them now," he said shakily. "They're fine."

"What were you doing up on that bridge?" Pearl snapped at me.

"I was . . . I was . . ." I looked over at Winnie. "I was daring Rita."

Rita and I flashed glances at each other. She looked terrified.

"Whatever possessed you?" Pearl's voice poked me like a spear. There was an uncomfortable silence.

Mr. Pulumbo cleared his throat. "There's something we need to talk about," he said. "Rita told us that Winnie pushed Virginia over the bank. I don't . . . we don't want to believe such a thing of Winnie, but we thought it should be discussed."

Pearl sucked in her breath. Winnie looked stunned.

"No." My father's voice flew like sand across the room, all gritty and rough. "That can't be true. Winnie ran to get me as soon as she saw Bryn climb up that railing. She had to have seen my truck and come right away. If she hadn't, I might not have been able . . . to get . . ." His voice ground out.

Pearl's face was terrible to look at, but Winnie looked directly at the Pulumbos.

"I didn't even see Winnie," I said. I remembered my perch on the bridge, saw again Virginia sliding toward the water. Thinking of it made me want to be sick.

"You know," my father started over, "Winnie had

100

the presence of mind to go get Leila Barton after she left me. She was thinking more clearly than almost anyone else today."

Pearl pressed her cheek against Winnie's head.

The Pulumbos looked at each other. "We had to know the truth," Dr. Pulumbo said.

"Not push Virginia," Winnie said matter-of-factly. "No, Pearl." She turned and touched her mother's face.

"I'm sorry," Dr. Pulumbo said, starting to cry again. She waved her hand weakly at Winnie. "Thank you. Thank you."

Pearl's voice shook. "If you're sure—"

"Oh, Pearl, Winnie didn't push anybody. Give the girl credit for being the only sensible soul down there today," my father said.

Pearl nodded, grabbed hold of Winnie's hand.

Everyone stared at Rita. Her mother hit her shoulder and said in a loud, abrasive voice, "Well? Did the retard push the little girl or not? Speak up!"

Rita shrugged away. She muttered something.

"What did you say?" Mrs. Pisgah shouted. "Speak up!"

"Maybe not," Rita shouted at her mother. Her eyes were filled with anger. "Nobody here is going to believe me, anyway," she sneered, standing up. Her mother made a snorting sound.

"I think you need to do something about her," Mrs. Pisgah said, pointing to Winnie's heart. "Come on, Rita." She pushed Rita toward the door, blowing into her handkerchief once more. As Rita disappeared into the night outside, Mrs. Pisgah turned back into the room.

"You needn't think she'll be sitting for you anymore," she said to the Pulumbos. She slammed the door.

"We thought Rita would have a better chance if we had her watch the girls," Mr. Pulumbo said to Pearl.

To my surprise, Pearl nodded.

"Poor Rita," said Leila, softly.

"Son ..." Mr. Pulumbo began hesitantly, then stopped and offered Cecil his hand. Cecil shook it, still looking at the floor. Leila didn't let go of his other hand. Dr. Pulumbo kissed him and hugged him. Cecil's face was scarlet.

The Pulumbos shook my father's hand, then Pearl's. Dr. Pulumbo stood in front of me, staring down. I curled deeper into the rocking chair.

"I guess ... Bryn," she said. She looked like she was going to haul me out of that chair and cry all over me. I shrank into the quilt. "Thank you," she said, wiping her hands across her cheeks. She went to Winnie, kissed her, and hugged her. Because Winnie was still attached to Pearl like a shield, Pearl got hugged, too. Then the Pulumbos left with Cecil, Frances, and Leila.

Pearl went upstairs with Winnie. My father and I were alone. He pulled me out of my chair and looked down into my face, his hands on my shoulders. He wasn't smiling.

"What you did today was foolish," he said. "Foolish and very, very dangerous. It's just lucky that things turned out the way they did."

102

I didn't know what to say. I felt bad. My father was right. Virginia and Rita could have been killed. Even Cecil could have been hurt.

"I'm so angry with you, Bryn," my dad said, "that I can hardly speak." He nudged me toward the stairs, but my feet were too heavy to climb up to my room. He started to roll a cigarette. His hands were shaking.

"Please," he said, without looking up. "Don't ever take such a risk again. I couldn't bear to lose you, not like that."

Until he said it, I hadn't thought about dying at all. It hadn't occurred to me before that I could have been killed, too.

"I'm sorry, Dad." I could feel tears swimming up to my eyes, but there had already been too much crying that night. I tried to push them down, and turned toward him.

"I'm glad you're okay," he said.

"I won't do it again."

"No." He was quiet a moment, rolling his cigarette. Then he said, "Just to help you remember, I'm not going to let you go to the Metcalfe Fair. You'll stay home and tend the house, and Pearl and Winnie will have a day to themselves without you."

I could feel a few tears leaking out of my eyes. I rubbed at them. "Okay, Dad," I said.

"I love you, Bryn," my father said, coming close and hugging me suddenly. He pulled a rough finger across my cheek. Then he went outside.

DREAM

I AM ALONE IN THE CORNFIELD.
I turn around and around, slowly, peering down each row.
Everywhere slim streets of dirt stretch out like giant brown
fingers among the stalks of green corn. Fat cobs swell from
the stems like presents.

Where is she? Where is my mother?

My eyes burn with tears, and I look up into the sky. It
is blue, a blue without clouds. Wait, there is a flash of
yellow in the corn, far down the field.

I want to go and see, but I cannot move from the spot
where I stand. My feet are rooted in mud.

"Come back! Come back! I'll be good. Please come
back." I cannot call her, because I am crying hard.

Winnie leans down.

"Bryn?" She is sleepy and tall in her green night-gown, a gentle stalk of a girl in my room. She holds a limp clown doll.

"Bryn?" She pushes at me, and I turn away, rolling

toward the wall. Winnie climbs in beside me, pulling the hem of her nightgown about her ankles. She curls around me like a spoon and is asleep. I turn my head to look at her.

The clown doll rests beneath her head like a small pillow. She sleeps with her mouth open. I close my eyes again. My face is damp against the sheets.

14

RITA wasn't at school the next day. All the kids in my classroom stared at me when I walked in and through the morning exercises, but no one said anything about what had happened at the bridge. Mrs. Fields pulled me aside at lunchtime.

"I don't think there's a need to take this event any further, do you, Bryn?" she said.

"No, ma'am." She squeezed my shoulder. She looked like she wanted to say more, but she just chewed her lip, nodded, and let me go.

"How about a bike ride after school?" Ed asked when I came out of the classroom.

"Sure," I said. "Where do you want to go?"

"I'll show you around some of Kenmore's back roads, okay? Meet me at the general store around three-thirty," he said easily. He dipped his head under his fine white hair and loped away from me.

"Okay," I said to the empty schoolyard. Ed moved fast when he wanted to be somewhere.

. . .

I was slinging on my knapsack when Pearl walked into the kitchen.

"Where are you off to?" she asked.

"Bike."

"Chores done?" Her eyes were traveling around the room.

"Yes."

"Outside, too?"

"Yes, Pearl. The wood is stacked, and the porch is swept," I said, heading for the door.

"Who are you going with?" Pearl asked, holding me with her blue eyes. It must have sounded like Twenty Questions, even to her, because she shrugged when she asked.

"Ed."

"Reece? Ed Reece? Oh," she said. "Well, then . . . be home to help with supper." She turned away.

I flew out the door and onto the bike. I glanced back and was surprised to see Pearl on the porch. She waved. I waved back.

Ed was waiting for me, and we rode along without speaking. Just past the school the road stops at a gravel crossroads. Ed turned right. Riding beside him in silence was comfortable. The sun shone through clouds scudding across the steel blue sky. The wind was crisp, but only my nose and cheeks felt cool. There were farms here and there along the road, but they were spaced far apart. All I could see were flat fields and a few falling-down, abandoned barns.

A few miles later Ed stopped.

"Need a rest?"

"Not really." I felt loose and warm and full of energy. Ed's heavy blue sweater and my red one were the brightest colors on the road. Ed took a jar of apple juice from his pack and offered me some. It was cold and sweet.

"Where are we going?" I asked.

"Nowhere in particular." He took off.

I followed more slowly, letting my bike fall some way behind his. We rode that way for a while.

"Hey, wait a minute," I called. Ed circled back to me. "This looks like the back of Pearl's farm."

Ed nodded. "Yes, it is," he said. "Want to turn in?"

"Sure," I said. "There's something I want to show you."

We dumped the bikes against the side of a tree and started into the woods. At first I wasn't sure where we were, but as we got further in, I recognized the tiny sugar shack in the distance. I took Ed over to show him Margaret Pearl's grave.

"I didn't know this was here," he said, reading the words. "It's sad, thinking of that guy leaving his family here all alone."

"There was a small cemetery on Island Road, just up from my house in Circleville," I told him. "My mother and I used to walk there. Some of the inscriptions on the gravestones were impossible to read, they were so old."

"Did you go there often?" Ed asked.

"Yes."

108

"Isn't that kind of a strange place to go walking?"

"Not really. It's not scary at all. There were less than thirty stones, sitting on a small hill up from a road like this one. Standing there, you could look down on fields stretching out from three sides. The families were people named Bowsher and Hoover. There was a soldier buried there from the War of 1812, and mothers, brothers, sisters, husbands, wives, and children."

"Hmm," said Ed. "It's sad."

"Well," I said, "my mother didn't think so."

"How about you?" he asked.

"I think it's a way of remembering people," I said slowly.

"You must really miss your mother, Ohio," Ed said softly.

"I do." There was no gravestone to mark my mother's place, but I remembered her.

"Do you want to talk about what happened?" Ed asked, pulling a loaf of bread, some cheese, and the apple juice out of his knapsack. He spread them out under a big tree.

For the first time since coming to Kenmore, I felt I could talk about it. "My mother walked into a cornfield and died," I told him. "One day, while I was at school, she just walked away and didn't come back. For nearly a week we didn't even know what had happened to her."

"I'm sorry," Ed said, looking at me quietly.

"We knew—and she knew—that she was very ill. But . . ." The next part was hard to say.

"But what?"

"She must have wanted to hurry things up," I said. "She didn't leave a note—she didn't say good-bye. I can't help wondering if I did something wrong, or if I could have done something different. . . ." Tears began to fill my throat, and I stopped talking.

Ed looked at me and sighed. He leaned against the tree and looked up at the sky. I could feel the tears backing away, and I looked up, too. The falcons were flying again, circling over Pearl's farm on the wind.

"Maybe when we die we don't really leave altogether," Ed said. "Maybe our spirits stay in a different form, or maybe just for a little while, until everything is taken care of. . . ." He began to rip apart the loaf of bread. He offered me a piece, and I chewed it slowly.

"Dad had her cremated," I said. "I don't even know where her ashes are."

We ate all the bread and cheese and some chocolate Ed found in his pocket. We packed up his knapsack again and sat awhile longer, until I began to feel cold.

"We better go back, Ed."

"Okay." As we pedaled, the afternoon grew colder. The sky had turned gray.

"Brrr. Pull over!" Ed called. "It smells like snow."

I sniffed the frosty air. There was a metallic edge to the wind now. My nose was running, and I couldn't find a tissue. Ed handed me a handkerchief.

I laughed. "I can't blow my nose in this," I told him.

"Why not?"

"Well, because . . . I don't know. It's yours. You won't want to put it back in your pocket after that."

110

"Right. You put it in your pocket," Ed agreed. "You can give it back to me another time. After you've washed it."

"Thanks!" I blew my nose. My eyes were watering, and my fingers were cold.

"Ohio." Ed was standing very close to me. The front wheel of his bike turned into mine. "Do girls like to kiss?"

"No," I told him, remembering Cecil's tuna fish lips. Ed looked disappointed. "Do boys?"

"I don't know," he said. He looked around as if expecting someone to appear on the road. No one did. "I think," he added, "that they do."

We looked at each other, shivering under the cold sky, wondering what to do about kissing.

"I'm really glad you saved Virginia," he said in a rush. "And I'm really glad you weren't hurt." I smiled.

"We better go," he told me, hopping on his bike. We rode fast the last few miles, warming ourselves in the rapidly darkening day.

"See ya," Ed called. He turned down the lane to his house, which I'd never seen, and went on without stopping.

"See ya," I called, but there was no one there.

By the time I got home, supper was steaming on the table and everyone was sitting down.

"You're—" Pearl began.

"I'm sorry I'm late," I said quickly. "We went further than we meant to go." I pulled off my sweater. The kitchen was warm, too warm, and I couldn't breathe properly.

"Where did you go?" My dad stood up and came over to me. "Bryn, your face is all red. Pearl?"

Pearl bustled over and put her hand on my forehead, then on my cheeks. My eyes felt like buttons sewed on to my face, stiff and heavy. "Fool goings-on," Pearl was muttering. "The girl has a raging fever. Winnie, run up and turn Bryn's bed down. David, bring tea." Snapping orders, she pushed me up the stairs and into the bathroom, where she stripped me down and scrubbed me with a cool washcloth.

I was too sleepy to do much about it. "Pearl! Pearl, don't."

"You're going right to bed," Pearl said firmly. "Arms up!"

I did what she told me, though she was treating me like a baby. As my nightgown came settling down over my head, I sneezed.

"Bed!" Pearl commanded, her hands nudging me gently into my room. She sat beside me and held out some tablets.

"I put lots of sugar in," Dad said, handing me a cup of tea.

I made a face, but I drank the hot, sweet liquid down in three gulps. I could feel it rushing through me. "Good," I mumbled.

Pearl tucked my quilt around my neck. Winnie stood uncertainly in the hall.

"Now, rest." Pearl took Winnie with her.

I was sliding into sleep like a runner heading for third base. "Dad," I whispered.

112

"Yes?"

"Where do boys learn how to kiss?"

"Same place girls do," he answered, stroking my cheek.

In my mind, I made it to home plate, but I may have been already asleep.

15

I woke up with a cold, but I didn't feel too bad and got dressed. It was late morning. I was surprised when Pearl came in with juice, toast, and tea on a big tray. A glass jar stuffed with leaves stood up in the middle of the food.

"Winnie's idea," said Pearl, catching my eye. "She's off at school."

Pearl watched me eat, then nodded and got up. "I guess you're fit enough," she said. "See you in the barn."

Always fit enough to work, I thought, but I was smiling.

We were cleaning stalls later when I heard Winnie.

"Baaaw!" Winnie sang as she approached, her eyes red and swollen. Her nose was running, and as we watched she pulled up the hem of her skirt to wipe it off.

"Winnie," Pearl said sharply. "Use your handkerchief."

Winnie patted her pockets feebly, but she didn't come up with anything. She came over to Pearl with her head down, mouth open, tears and nose streaming. She looked like a sick cow.

Pearl kneeled down.

"Retard!" she cried, falling on her knees and stuffing her head into Pearl's lap.

Pearl's body tightened. Her wrinkled hand came swiftly up to Winnie's hair and stroked it, very lightly.

"Who was it this time?" she asked quietly, but I knew.

"Rita, Rita call me retard," Winnie sobbed. There was silence in the barn. The animals were still out in the field, and now that I wasn't working I felt cold in there.

"You're not really retarded, Winnie," I said bravely, not sure if I meant it. I mean, Winnie wasn't completely normal, but if you lived with her for a while you certainly didn't think of her as retarded. I wanted her to stop crying. I wanted Pearl to say something. She did.

"Winnie is retarded," she said flatly. "It only means that she doesn't learn some things as fast as others do. She is different in the way she does some things. It's true. She is retarded."

Winnie looked up at Pearl. She wasn't crying now. For a moment it almost looked as if she hated Pearl. She pulled away, patting at her pockets again. She found the square of white cotton and blew her nose vigorously. "Mean," she said, not to anyone in particular.

Pearl grabbed Winnie and hugged her tight, tipping her puffy face up with her hand to look at her. "I'm sorry, Winnie," she said simply. "There's nothing we can do about the way you were born, except do our best to help you learn what you can. But Earl and I loved you before you were even born, and we ... I love you still. I always will. That's more than some kids ever have." She got up and left the barn.

"I'm sorry you're retarded, Winnie," I said. "It doesn't matter to me." What I said was true. I was used to Winnie now. I liked her the way she was.

"Pearl tell me all the time," Winnie said.

"She does?"

"Yes. I have to work hard. Learn to take care of myself," she said wistfully. Her face was filthy, and bits of straw clung to her hair.

"Does it make you feel bad?"

"Not when Pearl say," Winnie said. "When kids stare, when Rita say retard, I cry."

"Rita's stupid, anyway," I said. "You shouldn't care what she says."

I wondered why Pearl didn't say something to Rita, or maybe to Mrs. Pisgah. I asked her that night at supper.

"Many of the things Rita says she hears at home," Pearl said. "Besides, I can't be with Winnie all the time, and I can't change the whole world just by wishing it. I try to help Winnie feel good about herself. The truth is, after that, it's up to Winnie."

"Rita doesn't have to go out of her way to make Winnie feel bad," I said.

"Sometimes I guess you can feel so bad yourself, you can't notice how others might feel." Pearl left the table.

116

I decided to speak to Winnie, anyway.

"Rita Pisgah better not say any more mean things to you when I'm around," I told her that night when we were getting ready to go to bed. "If she bothers you anymore, you just tell her I'll fix her wagon."

Winnie smiled. "Wagon?" she said.

"Never mind," I said. "She just better not call you names anymore."

I couldn't breathe very well, and it was hard to fall asleep that night. After lying awake for what seemed like hours, I decided to get up. I opened my bedroom door and stopped to listen. Soft light was coming from Dad's room. I tiptoed in that direction.

His door was open, and he was sitting at a small desk, almost identical to the one in my room. There were envelopes and papers all over, and my father was propped on his elbows, his hands covering his face. He must have heard me gasping for air, because he looked up. His face was wet, his eyes red and tired looking. My father was crying.

"What's wrong, honey?" he said in a hoarse voice.

"Oh, Dad." I hesitated in the doorway for a moment. I'd never seen my father cry. He held open his arms, and I went to him. We hugged.

"I just came to say good-night," I said, almost shy.

"Good-night." Dad kissed my cheek and tried to smile.

I walked slowly to my room, then turned around. In a moment Dad's light went out. I got into my bed and went right to sleep. I didn't even dream.

117

16

SATURDAY morning, Dad greeted me cheerfully as he went out to do his chores. It seemed that everyone in Kenmore was thinking about the Metcalfe Fair, and everyone was going, except me. Pearl left me only the kitchen to clean and some weeding to do. She told me to wear a sweater.

"Don't mind the cows," she said. "We'll be back for milking. You can get supper started and set the table."

Winnie looked behind her as they left, but I just waved. I tried not to care that I was missing the fair.

My dad came in. "I've got to run out to Smiths' place," he said, "and then I thought I'd take a quick look at the fair."

For a moment I thought he was going to change his mind about me, but he just gave me a kiss and left.

I did the stuff Pearl asked me to do, then curled up with a book in the old chair outside, with an old handkerchief of Pearl's and a bowl of oranges. Ed had given me the story of King Arthur to read, and it was really good. The sun flickered across the pages of my book. I nibbled, blew my nose, and then I guess I went to sleep.

I woke up feeling chilly and went to put more wood into Pearl's stove. I gobbled down a cucumber sandwich. Pearl makes hers with mayonnaise, but I slapped some mustard on mine and cut the cucumber into thick slices. I set the table and put the stewpot Pearl had readied for me on the back of the stove with the kettle.

Walking around that empty house gave me a peaceful feeling. I waltzed into the living room to look through Pearl's books, but it was cold in there, and I wandered back into the kitchen. I decided to sweep off the porch and fill a bowl of apples from the basement storage for the table, as a kind of centerpiece. I stuck in some brilliant leaves from the yard. It looked pretty.

I didn't plan to, but the next thing I found myself doing was walking into my father's bedroom and standing over his desk. The mess of papers had been tidied up a little and folded into a pile with a rubber band snapped around them. I ripped the band from the papers and unfolded letter after letter from the stack. Every single one of them started with the line "Dear Julia."

A trembling began in my chest and ran swiftly through all of my bones. It seemed Dad was writing my mother letters just about every day. I put most of them back into a pile, but I opened the one that had been on the top.

"Dear Julia," I read. "Our Bryn is growing tall, changing as fast as the seasons change. You would be delighted with your girl, so brave and busy. She wants

119

to stay here, wants to make Pearl and Winnie our family. It's just so hard for me to promise her, because when I look up, wherever I am, from whatever it is I am doing, I still expect to see you. It is still such a shock to see others standing where I think you will be."

Pearl's truck chugged into the yard, with my father's right behind it.

With shaking hands I refolded the letter and wound the band around the papers again. I raced downstairs.

Winnie ran into the kitchen. "You won prize!" she shouted, waving her arms. "Bryn, you are third prize for Rita!"

"What?"

"She's telling you, girl, you won third prize for your poster in the accident prevention contest, though I don't know what Rita has to do with it," Pearl said. "Mrs. Fields will give you the ten dollars' prize money next week. Congratulations."

I grinned at Winnie.

"Rita," she repeated. "Whee-ha!"

My dad walked in, smiling. "I'm proud of you, Bryn. Here, I brought a small piece of the fair to you." He handed me some cotton candy on a paper cone. It was a bit melted, but the pink sugar tasted fine.

Although it was only October, it started to get cold, especially at night. The leaves were already changing from rich gold and scarlet to drab, wrinkled brown. I was surprised to hear that Canadians have their

Thanksgiving a whole month earlier than it's celebrated in the States. Pearl got busy cooking up several large turkeys. Winnie and I made pies under her supervision, and I rolled dough until my arms ached.

"What do we need so many pies for, anyway?" I asked, glaring at the apple, mince, pumpkin, meat, lemon, pecan, cherry, and peach-filled shells.

Pearl didn't bother to answer. She just sent me to the pantry for her cranberry cake recipe.

The stove roared day after day and far into the night, turning Pearl's loaves and buns a toast color. The smells lingered through the days like perfume. I almost couldn't eat, I was so full of smelling.

When the big day came, Pearl sent Winnie and me through the village with an old wagon, which she loaded with pies and bread and whole plates of sliced meat. She handed us a list of places to visit with a note beside each name, telling us what to leave.

It was cold, but we warmed up fast pulling that heavy wagon. Winnie sang and slapped her hands together while I pulled. When it was her turn, I stuck my hands deep into the pockets of my jacket and tipped my head back to the sky. I walked backward for a while, then danced up the lane ahead of her, but she just laughed and said, "Oh, Bryn."

We visited a lot of old people, more than I knew even lived in Kenmore. Winnie seemed to know them all, although few of them said anything to her. She solemnly handed each one Pearl's gift. Some of them just said thank you and went right back into their houses. One old woman started talking to Winnie, then stopped abruptly, shook her head, and slammed the door. A couple of them stared at me.

I took a platter of meat up to one door and got a grumpy old man with a purple nose. "Pearl MacDonald'll give me heartburn again this year." He laughed a little, but with trembling hands he took the plate from me and the pie Winnie offered. I peeked behind him into a dark room. There was one dim light on. It seemed almost as cold in his house as it was outside.

We both took pies to Leila. Cecil was playing with Frances on the rug. Winnie bent down to pat Frances's chubby hands, but it was almost evening and we had to go home.

"Tell Pearl thank you," said Leila softly. She was stirring a pot of chicken soup, and there was a loaf of bread on the table, but that's all there was to eat that I could see.

Walking back down the lane, I realized that it must be hard for Leila to feed herself, Frances, and Cecil. I knew she sewed for some of the local women, but she had baby Frances to care for as well. Cecil worked at the general store every day after school and on Saturday. That couldn't be for "extra" money, the way Pearl and even Cecil had suggested. They needed the money to eat.

Our own table was loaded with food. Pearl had set out the good silver on a red tablecloth, and served corn with the potatoes and turkey. There were lots of other vegetables, breads, and desserts to choose from, along with the usual milk and tea.

Mike peeked boldly from Winnie's apron pocket. She was feeding him crumbs right from her fingers, and Pearl didn't say a thing.

When Pearl started praying, I suddenly thought of the old man in his silent house and Leila in her small kitchen.

" 'Let the heavens be glad, and let the earth rejoice: and let men say among the nations, the Lord reigneth,' " Pearl read from her Bible. " 'Let the sea roar, and the fullness thereof: let the fields rejoice, and all that is therein. Then shall the trees of the wood sing out at the presence of the Lord, because he cometh to judge the earth. O give thanks unto the Lord, for he is good; for his mercy endureth forever.' " She looked up. "Amen," she prompted.

"Amen," we said, and we started to eat.

"Won't you have a roll?" Pearl asked. "You made these."

I didn't recognize it, but I ate a roll and lots besides; then when I was in my bed feeling stuffed and warm and safe, I thought again about the people we had visited with the wagon. Suddenly the pile of food Pearl had given away seemed small in the face of their hunger. For the first time in my life, I understood that being alive doesn't automatically guarantee you enough to eat.

17

IN November my father volunteered to help Cecil fix the roof of the Barton house. Ed and his father said they were going to help, too.

"Should have been done long before this cold weather," my father grumbled the morning he was getting ready to go.

"No one had time before," Pearl said crisply.

"That boy has too much responsibility," my father said. "Works too hard for a kid." He never seemed to worry about the work Pearl made me do.

Pearl handed him a basket of things to eat. I knew that for today, at least, Cecil would be full of food. "Leila and the baby will come down here," Pearl told my father. "If it gets too cold, get off the roof and get warm, for heaven's sake."

"We'll be fine, Pearl," Dad said impatiently. I knew they would all be back for the evening meal.

Leila, Frances, and Mrs. Reece, Ed's mother, all arrived together. They had their sewing, and Winnie played with Frances. I was using the paints my father had given me to color in some sketches. They were turning out pretty well.

The women were laughing.

"What's so funny?" I asked.

They smiled, but did not answer.

I decided to go outside with Winnie and Frances for a while. When we came back in, Winnie made tea and Leila nursed Frances. Pearl whisked around the kitchen, making lunch. I started setting the table.

"Ed's grown out of a lot of his things, Leila," said Mrs. Reece. "Will you look through them and take anything you think Cecil might use?"

Leila flushed, but she nodded. "Thank you, Sheryl."

"I'll just be fighting off a cloud of moths all winter if I keep them," Mrs. Reece said lightly. "I have no more boys, and the clothes won't do anybody good in the closet."

"Your children are mighty fortunate," Pearl said to her.

"Yes, they are," Mrs. Reece said. "And so are yours." It felt funny to be included as one of Pearl's children. She looked over at me and grinned. I couldn't smile back.

My dad returned early to do the milking and took Winnie with him to the barn. Everyone else came stomping in around five, laughing and talking. Ed's face was bright red. When Cecil pulled his woolen cap off, his hair stuck straight up in the air, crackling.

I helped put dinner on the table. Cecil and Ed rounded up extra chairs. Pearl had whipped up a roasted ham, baked potatoes, and boiled squash. There was the usual tea and lots of pie all around. When Winnie and Dad got back from their chores, everyone was sitting at the table.

We ate and ate until finally my father cried, "Whoa!" and got up. People were talking. Winnie was busy keeping up with Frances. The baby crawled around the kitchen, under the table and out again and down the hall to the living room. She was as quick as a puppy. Winnie's face was red and happy as she bent and scooped and let Frances go, over and over again.

I watched my dad playing checkers with Cecil. Cecil beat him three times; then I played a game. You have to think fast if you take on Cecil Barton, and I was out of practice. He won every game, but it was fun.

My father and Leila were laughing about something at the table. Pearl was making more tea.

"Your knees hurting?" Ed asked Cecil.

"Naw."

"Mine are," Mr. Reece said, grimacing.

"Bryn, put your coat on and take these out to the horses," said Pearl, pulling a basket of peelings and spoiled fruit to the door. "Dump the rest on the manure pile. And bring in those milking jackets from the hook. They must smell to high heaven by now."

I was glad when Ed said, "I'll help you," shrugging on his coat and grabbing one end of the basket. We walked through the crisp air to the barn.

"I don't know why you'd want to help me do this . . ." I began. The sweet odor of peelings rose from

126

the basket between us. Pearl had slopped the bruised apples and some small carrots on top, and Ed filled his pockets with them.

"I like you, Ohio," he said. We walked to the manure heap first and heaved the contents of the basket into it.

"Lucky it's too cold to smell much," I said.

Ed smiled. It was warm in the barn. The horses wrapped their lips around the apples and lifted them gently from our palms before crushing them in their great, flat teeth.

"I better get those jackets," I said then, heading for the door.

"Wait," said Ed. He pulled me close to him. I could feel his heart banging against his chest. I was standing on his foot, and my hand was jammed against the wall.

"What?" I said.

Ed just looked at me.

"I'm going to kiss you," he said, and before I could tell him that girls really don't like to kiss, he did it. He put his mouth very gently on mine and rubbed his lips softly along the edge of my cheeks and back to my mouth. His breath didn't smell of anything but apples. Much nicer than tuna fish.

I found out girls do like to kiss. It just depends on who they're kissing. The feeling a kiss gives you doesn't stay in your face—it flies around your body.

"Boys," said Ed, "do like kissing."

"Where are those jackets?" Pearl wanted to know when we came back to the house.

"I didn't see them," I told her. It was true. I had forgotten.

Later, Pearl made popcorn and cocoa, and we sat around the kitchen table together, talking. I didn't mention getting kissed to anyone, not even Winnie. Somehow, a good kiss is a lot more private than a tuna fish kiss.

It snowed the next day. I watched for hours as the thick white stuff piled up on the big tree outside. It hardly ever snowed in Circleville. I had never seen so much come down at one time. It was lovely. Snow does have a smell, a clean, light smell that seemed to drift through the thin glass of Pearl's windows and fill the rooms with cold.

Winnie and I climbed into piles of clothes and played outside like little kids. We made snowballs, snow angels, snowmen, and snow women. Winnie even made snow mice. We ate the snow, threw the snow, and plunged through it like workhorses. When we dragged ourselves back inside, we were exhausted. Pearl made us change into our nightgowns and sit by the stove. We had hot soup for supper.

I couldn't believe how happy I felt. Winnie's cheeks were pink, and she fell asleep in the rocking chair. Pearl gave me some shelf paper, and I tried to draw a picture of Winnie. It didn't turn out very well. I tried a few still-life sketches. The one I made of Pearl's teapot looked pretty good. Pearl hung it up on the refrigerator.

128

The snow kept on falling in Kenmore. We had exams in school.

By December, snow was piled high along the roads. My father kept the path to the barn clear, but Pearl gave me the job of keeping the porch and steps open to the road and each morning sent me out there before breakfast. She also started serving oatmeal with our tea and toast. Shoveling put me in a sweat on even the coldest mornings.

Snow was coming down again when Winnie and I trudged home from school on the Wednesday before Christmas break. Pearl was in the kitchen.

"Drat!" she said, kicking the woodbox. Her breath smoked in the air. "Stove's out," she said. "I stayed out in the barn too long today." She looked through the window. It was already getting dark. "Winnie, bring in wood so I can light the stove. Bryn, stop staring and get the soup out of the fridge."

We went to work, leaving on our coats and hats. It didn't take long to get the stove roaring and the soup on, but it was still cold in there. Pearl tucked leftovers in a pan and put them in the oven. Winnie and I set the table with our mittens on, blowing puffs of breath at each other.

My father came in stamping his feet and clapping his mittened hands against his chest.

"Dinner isn't ready," Pearl said. "Let's go on a night walk."

We trudged through the dark to the bridge. The sky was black, but snow reflects a lot of light. I could see

Pearl in the lead. She walked firmly across her land. She knew where we were and where we were going. There was Winnie, tall behind her, leaping easily through the drifts. My dad followed, his head down against the wind, stomping along after them.

The three of them in the snow looked so familiar. It was strange to be left behind, standing still for a moment at the end of the line. I felt forgotten, and then my father turned and waved at me. I waved back. He waited for me to catch up.

"Should we stay, Bryn?" he asked as I reached him.

"Stay?"

"Stay, yes, let's stay," he said.

"Here, you mean?" I grinned, waving my arm in the darkness toward Pearl's farm.

"Yes," he said.

"Okay." I put my mittened hand in his and ducked my face into my scarf for warmth. We waded through the snow after Pearl and Winnie.

Mrs. Fields had read us a poem in which winter is described as the barren heart of the year, a bleakness of the soul. She said poets usually plan things so that winter stands for death and sorrow, and spring represents new life and joy. Standing in that muffled night, I felt differently.

I knew that inside the cold night was Pearl's warm house. We would go back there. The stove would warm our faces. The dinner would smell good. Inside the winter, spring was growing. I was growing too, growing a new heart, just as Pearl said people do.

DREAM

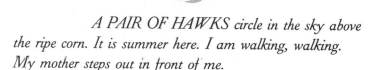

  *A PAIR OF HAWKS circle in the sky above
the ripe corn. It is summer here. I am walking, walking.
My mother steps out in front of me.*

 *She puts her arms around me and hugs me. Her brown
curls shine in the sun. I stroke her hair and take a deep
breath, smelling her skin. She holds me a long time.*

 *She kisses my face and steps back. She is wearing her
red dress. "I love you," she says.*

 "I love you," I tell her.

 Then she is gone.

 *Now I walk through the field. I come to the last row of
corn. I push through the tall, dry leaves and stand in grass,
looking up at the hawks. I can see our old house, I can
see horses running in the pasture, I can see the barn and
Island Road rolling around the curve behind the next field.
Someone else must live here now.*

 *I know I will not come back. I lift my hand to wave,
and the horses raise their heads to me. This is good-bye.*